The WICKETT SISTERS
In Heaven

The
WICKETT
SISTERS
In Heaven

STEPHEN HOUSER

A Novel by Stephen Houser

This is a work of fiction. Names, characters, places,
and incidents either are the product of the author's imagination
or are used fictitiously.
Any resemblance to actual persons, living or dead,
events, or locales is entirely coincidental.

First Printing

Hardcover ISBN: 978-1-68564-009-5

Cover Art and Design by Vincent Chong

With love and appreciation,
this Wickett Sisters adventure is dedicated to
Peter R. Haggard
and
Lorraine Mardell Petrakis
early supporters, and yes, Lorraine
is that Mardie

CHAPTER ONE

G abriel is dead.

Mili opened her eyes. The townhouse bedroom was dark. Her husband Lucifer was sleeping peacefully at her side, his back snuggled against hers.

Gabriel is dead.

Mili lay without moving. Had she heard someone say it? Here? In her dreams?

Gabriel is dead.

During Mili's years as an inspector at Scotland Yard she had often dreamed about her investigations, her mind sifting through case details, winnowing her dreams for the motives and deeds of thieves, murderers, rapists, traitors, spies, and felons of every description. And very often her night investigations actually sorted out the most likely villain.

Mili smelled cigarette smoke. She looked at the alarm clock on her bed stand. Four o'clock. The hour that beckoned the troubled from their sleep to lie awake and worry until dawn. In this case it was Sriracha's nicotine habit that had nudged *him* awake. He was twelve and he smoked all the time. Little Mardie was eighteen and had never put a cigarette between her lips. Jesus, who was seven years old now, prayed for his brother Sriracha and hung anti-smoking posters in his bedroom.

Even though smoking in Hell didn't come with the health risks it threatened on Earth—chronic coughing, raw throats, creeping emphysema, debilitating COPD, and deadly lung cancer—it was still a filthy habit. Sriracha smoked endlessly, filling his bedroom with smoke. It made his breath perpetually sour and coated his fingers with yellow nicotine stains.

Sriracha was not allowed to smoke anywhere in the house except in his bedroom. However, since he chain-smoked cigarettes all day long—and woke up periodically to smoke at night—no one who'd ever been in his smoky room went back. Any more than a World War I veteran would voluntarily venture back into the mustard gas of no man's land.

Mili got out of bed, pulled on a long silk robe, and used the restroom in the master bedroom. Then she walked down the hall to Sriracha's room. She noticed that the lights were on, glowing beneath the door. She knocked softly.

"Sriracha?"

"Yes, Mom?" he answered.

"Would you like to have some milk and cookies with me in the kitchen?"

"Sure!"

"Mouthwash first, little love," Mili told him. "See you shortly."

She turned on a hall light and went downstairs. Mili decided to brew a cup of tea and put on the kettle. She set out a plate full of Oreos for her son and filled a large glass with cold milk. She stood by the stove and set out a teacup holding a Twinings tea bag, a bowl of sugar, and the carton of milk she had used to fill Sriracha's glass.

Her son appeared in the kitchen doorway. He had slipped on a white T-shirt and jeans, and not only had he used mouthwash, he had brushed his teeth as well. He was a handsome young man with a gorgeous aquiline nose, sparkling amber eyes, and a square jaw with a deep dimple in his chin. He had his father's curly blond hair. But whereas Lucifer wore his in waves down his shoulders, Sriracha wore it short on the sides and back and gelled the top into a tall corkscrew fauxhawk.

"Hi, honey," she said.

Sriracha smiled happily.

Mili beckoned him with her finger.

"Mama needs some sugar," she told him.

He laughed and came over and hugged her. He only came up to her chin, but that would surely pass. She wrapped him close and kissed his forehead. He sat down and grabbed a handful of Oreos. He pulled them apart one at a time. He ate the frosting, then consumed the chocolate cookies. He had no idea how the whole cookie tasted all together. Neither did Mili. She ate Oreos the same way her son did.

Mili filled her teacup with hot water, milk, and several spoons of sugar. Then she sat down at the kitchen table.

"Did you wake up to have a smoke?" she asked her son.

Sriracha took a big drink of milk and then answered.

"No," he said softly. "A voice woke me up. I thought it was you."

"In the middle of the night?"

"I know!" Sriracha said. "It got me totally worried."

"What did you hear?" Mili asked.

Sriracha frowned. Then he spoke.

"Gabriel is dead."

Mili was shocked, but hid her surprise.

"Honey, I couldn't have said that," she responded gently. "I was sleeping."

Sriracha frowned.

"Well, *someone* said it. I told you it woke me up."

Mili watched Sriracha undial a few Oreos and down them. She didn't tell her son that she thought she had heard the same exact words that he had. Gabriel is dead. Didn't make any sense that both of them had heard it. She gazed at Sriracha. He looked beat. And, truth be told, anxious and worried as well.

"Are you going to be too tired for school today?" she asked.

Sriracha's face grew suddenly hopeful.

"Maybe," he said, willing to consider the possibility that he might not have to attend his tutoring sessions. He was home schooled on weekdays. So were Little Mardie and Jesus.

Mili watched Sriracha eat his cookies and drink his milk.

"You don't really like home school, do you, sweet?" she asked. He had, in fact, complained about his studies often, but Mili was determined that his days wouldn't just be filled with video games and endless cigarettes.

"What's your point, Mom?" Sriracha asked.

"Most of the new jobs down here require training," Mili told him. "The kibbutz will be building schools for all ages and a university will certainly be planned as well." Sriracha gazed at her, wondering how any of that applied to him. "Your own sister Little Mardie is already planning to go to high school as soon as it opens."

"Yes, but she's marrying a kibbutznik and both of them want to learn about farming," Sriracha pointed out.

"Indeed," Mili agreed. "Won't that be wonderful?"

Little Mardie had been together for several years now with a Jewish boy named Arie Millatiner who lived and worked at the kibbutz. She was eighteen—all grown up really—and still lived in the Morningstar flat at the kibbutz. Marriage plans were being made, but no date had been set.

"I'm not interested in being a farmer," Sriracha protested. "I don't like even being outside. I don't want to spend my life picking fruit. Or raising animals."

"What *do* you want to do?" Mili asked, getting up and fetching another plate full of Oreos. Not so long ago, Hell was poor and sad.

Now it offered opportunity and challenges. While most of perdition's old timers were content to just drink and fornicate, the most recent arrivals joined the generation of residents who had been born here in pursuing careers, sports, travel, and socializing. You could be what you wanted to be.

"I like drawing," Sriracha told his mother.

"And you're brilliant at it," Mili told him proudly. Sriracha loved reading about T.T. Sutherland's dragon adventures and Erin Hunter's warrior cats. He'd drawn hundreds of dragons and cats to perfection. And now at twelve, he'd begun drawing people in earnest though his women were portrayed as thin and flat-chested. He wouldn't be getting a job drawing female superheroes at Marvel anytime soon.

"I want to be a graphic novelist," Sriracha said.

"That would be wonderful!" Mili said, thrilled that her son was thinking of a real occupation that required talent and hard work.

"But," Sriracha asked, "how would I get my work published? Not to mention there aren't any bookstores in Hell."

"There will be," Mili replied confidently. "There are franchise talks already about a bookstore chain happening at the bank already, and I wouldn't mind investing in it myself. Plus, if Jeff Bezos winds up down here you'll see as many Amazon bookstores as Starbucks shops."

Lucifer had negotiated directly with Starbucks Chairman Howard Schultz on Earth to get him to open a chain of Starbucks in Hell. A pious and moral Jew Schultz had hesitated. When the Devil had David Ben-Gurion and Moshe Dayan describe to him the Devil's efforts to improve Hell, Schultz got on board. Now there were Starbucks *and* Ben and Jerry's everywhere down here. Coffee and ice cream. Did anyone really need more than that?

"If you are certain that you want to do graphic novels," Mili told Sriracha, "I'll talk to your father about switching your home studies to art." Sriracha looked thrilled. Mili went on. "It's a craft that requires technique and discipline. It's a calling that will eventually require you to get formal schooling. Just so you know, lots of art classes will be offered in the new kibbutz high school."

"Little Mardie told me that," Sriracha said. "She and Arie are signing up for agriculture courses, but Arie is also going to take a watercolor painting class. David Ben-Gurion got permission from Heaven to have Marc Chagall teach down here for a semester. Arie loves his work. He says Chagall is a proud Jew who paints with the heart of a Christian."

Mili raised her eyebrows. She had seen Chagall's splendid stained glass windows in Jerusalem. He had portrayed Jewish lore in wonderful images, but she hadn't noticed anything remotely Christian about his work.

"Does Arie have interest in Christian themes?"

"Well, strictly speaking, I'd say that his interest is limited to Chagall's images of Christ," Sriracha replied. "He painted a lot of scenes of his crucifixion. Arie told me there was even a book about those paintings, filled with green crosses and yellow Jesus's. Pretty wild stuff."

Mili stared at her son. What amazing things were hidden in his mind? These were revelations that she had never even supposed might be in her boy's thoughts. She felt embarrassed that she had not taken the time to explore them with her oldest son until now.

"If you write down the name of that book, I'll get a copy for you," she told him. "You could show me the pictures you like."

Sriracha's face lit up.

"Oh, thank you, Mom!"

He jumped up and gave Mili a great big hug.

"I have to go now," he said.

"Tired, my angel?" Mili asked.

"No. I need a smoke."

Mili chuckled, ruffled her son's hair, and sent him off. She decided to have another cup of tea, wanting to think a bit more about the life-changing conversation that she and Sriracha had just shared. Her son wanted to be a graphic novelist, creating both the stories and the art himself. He knew that the kibbutz high school would offer art courses. Arie was going to take one about watercolors. Taught by Marc Chagall himself. Who did yellow Jesus's on green crosses.

Mili loved being a mother. Her three children were so wonderful and each so different. Little Mardie was confident and verbal just like her namesake. Sriracha had the heart of an artist and the hands of a smoker. Jesus was tender and sweet, clearly a real angel. Yet what did she know of their thoughts and desires? They were healthy, well-fed, and cared about. But what had she ever really asked them to share?

It was a terrible failing on her part. How had she let it happen? Her parents had never asked her anything about anything. Her sister loved her to pieces, but had never probed her thoughts and feelings. And, of course, neither had Lucifer. Oh, they talked, but not intimately. Yet thoughts and feelings truly mattered. Look at everything she had just heard Sriracha reveal. My God. Stuff she would never have even guessed. Said a lot about where she had failed to use her investigative talents.

Mili finished her tea. Lucifer appeared in the kitchen doorway. He looked haggard. As if he hadn't slept well. He gave his wife a tired little wave.

"Hi, love," she told him. "Are you alright?"

Satan shook his head.

"Had a restless night," he replied. "I kept dreaming that someone died."

"Gabriel?" Mili asked softly.

Lucifer didn't answer. He just stared. Then he nodded.

CHAPTER TWO

L ucifer sat down at the kitchen table. Mili served him a cup of black coffee. He was wearing a white cotton robe and he'd combed out his long blond hair. It fell in waves over his shoulders. He took a drink of his coffee and looked at Mili's face. She sipped at her tea and waited for him to talk.

"Why did you mention Gabriel?" he asked, a wary look in his eye. He did not believe that Mili had read his mind. *Spoken* words were the currency of the kingdom of the damned, not thoughts. His own endless mental wanderings only became decipherable when he spoke them out loud. Streams of consciousness might work for novelists like James Joyce in *Ulysses*, but for everyone else they were genuine hooey until spoken out loud and analyzed.

"I was sleeping," Mili answered. "I heard—or dreamed I heard—someone say, 'Gabriel is dead.'"

Satan nodded.

"That may well have been me," he confessed. "I had a dream in which some person kept saying 'Gabriel is dead.' When I interrupted to ask how, or when, or under what circumstances, the person simply repeated 'Gabriel is dead.'"

Mili watched Lucifer. He was obviously perplexed, and though she would never mention it to him, he was clearly anxiety-ridden as well.

"Have you ever had an experience like this before?" she asked.

Lucifer rubbed his forehead as though trying to settle his thoughts. Then he replied.

"Once," he said in a subdued voice. "In the days that led up to the attempt to kill Jehovah, I dreamed every night that an angel came to me and told me that God was dead. Of course, he wasn't. My long history of misery wanted it to be true, but it was not."

Satan fell silent. Mili had heard Lucifer speak only once about Heaven's rebellion and his determination to assassinate God. She wondered if she would learn any more right now as Lucifer silently contemplated the meaning of this new dream. Gabriel is dead.

Mili had met Gabriel many times as Lucifer's guest in their previous house, now unfortunately burned to the ground. He had come for tea and cakes, British style, and had always seemed so kind and appreciative. Standing seven feet tall, he had fair skin and blue eyes, long, thick blond hair, and a beautiful face. His slim build belied the fact that his angelic body housed a strength that could move stars or destroy worlds. But those were not his tasks. He was God's messenger to men. He had been more active once upon a time than now. Jehovah had not seemed to have much to communicate to humankind the last couple of thousand years.

Mili had not met the other Archangels, Raphael and Michael. Raphael was God's

closest companion. Michael was Jehovah's hand of discipline, famously known for his massacres. Sodom and Gomorrah's entire populations. Hundreds of thousands of Assyrian soldiers encamped against Jerusalem. Millions of Soviet peasants who'd turned away from the Russian Orthodox Church. He was, to be fair, just as effective executing only a single person. Nimrod the Hunter. Julius Caesar. Alexander Hamilton. Napoleon Bonaparte.

Lucifer looked at her again.

"I have to go to Heaven and find out if Gabriel is indeed dead."

"Are you afraid for him??" Mili asked.

"I am," Lucifer replied softly. "He is always gracious to me. Never treats me like a castoff, even though, of course, I am. I always wanted to be like him. But I possess an anger and a violence that is more like Michael. So, sadly, Gabriel I am not. It will be very painful for me if that gentle and remarkable Archangel has indeed met his demise." Satan paused and frowned. "Mark my word, dear heart, I better not learn that either Jehovah or Michael destroyed Gabriel." Mili watched Lucifer intently, but he had nothing more to say. What he had spoken already, however, struck fear into the very depths of her heart.

✳ ✳ ✳

After Lucifer left, Mili called Mardie. It was only nine o'clock in the morning, but perhaps her sister was up early. She was. Mardie answered on the second ring. Her face looked stressed on Mili's iPhone screen.

"Bad time?" Mili asked.

"No," Mardie answered. "And good morning to you, too."

"Yes," Mili muttered. "Sorry. Good morning. You look upset."

"I am," Mardie confirmed. "Stayed up late watching the telly. Was laid out flat by the news bulletins that Gabriel is dead."

Mili felt faint. She sat down in a kitchen table chair.

"Which Gabriel?" She asked.

"Do you know a lot of them?" Mardie replied impatiently. "It was Gabriel the Archangel."

"He died in Heaven?"

"He was *murdered* in Heaven."

Mili couldn't speak. Couldn't respond. Couldn't even grasp that.

"How did it happen?" she finally got out.

"No one knows. Demons broke the news last night."

11

"But not to Lucifer."

"No one told the boss?"

"No. He had a premonition during the night, but nothing more than that. It was enough, however, to send him off to Heaven early this morning to investigate."

"Will you call me when you hear anything?"

"I will. I'm going to ask Pfot to take me and the family to the kibbutz this afternoon. I want to visit Little Mardie, and it turns out that Sriracha would very much like to know more about art classes being offered when the kibbutz high school opens."

"Good for him!" Mardie said.

"Want to come with us?" Mili asked. "You can have dinner and stay over."

"I'd like that," Mardie responded. "I think Little Mardie is old enough to hear some tales from her aunt's adventurous past."

"Don't you dare!" Mili said sharply.

"I promised her way back when," Mardie insisted.

"You're old," Mili shot back. "Tell her you forgot whatever you promised."

"She'll be missing out," Mardie warned.

"Oh, right. Smoking, drinking, one-night stands, and STDs."

"I *never* got a disease," Mardie said indignantly.

"She's not going to know that because you're not going to talk about it."

Mardie frowned, but didn't reply.

"We'll pick you up at ten o'clock."

"I'll be ready," Mardie said in an icy voice.

"Think of some *nice* stories to tell Little Mardie," Mili suggested.

"That might be hard to do," Mardie countered. "This is *my* life we're talking about."

"*Make up* a story then. You're a writer."

Mardie nodded happily.

"Now *that* I can do."

✳ ✳ ✳

These days it was no more than a half hour's drive from New Babylon to the Ben-Yehuda Kibbutz as the highway connecting them had been repaired and repaved. During the first part of today's trip everyone had listened to a CD that Jesus had asked Pfot to play. It was entitled *Plastic Beach* by a rock group called the Gorillaz. The music was mostly genteel and relaxing.

"There hasn't been anything quite like this since the glory days of the Grateful Dead," Sriracha commented. "When Jerry Garcia was still singing with them."

"Are we talking druggie music?" Mardie asked.

"What's druggie music?" Jesus asked. His face looked innocent, but it belied a mature and open mind for a seven-year-old.

"Any music that feels extra good when a person has taken a drug to relax and veg out," Sriracha told him.

"So, perhaps cannabis, opium, or salvia divinorum," Jesus commented.

Everyone in the car stared at him. Even Pfot, who used the rear-view mirror to do so.

"You forgot hashish," Sriracha told him.

"Hashish is just cannabis resin," Jesus responded.

"Really?" Sriracha reacted. "I didn't know that. But then I haven't tried any of the drugs you just rattled off."

"I haven't either," Jesus said somewhat indignantly. "Intelligent people don't do drugs." He looked at Sriracha sitting next to him in the back seat. "They don't smoke either."

Sriracha rolled his eyes. A gesture he had learned from his mother. Something neither she nor he *ever* did around Lucifer, who hated it.

"Why *do* you smoke?" Jesus asked his brother for the thousandth time.

13

"It helps me level up," Sriracha answered seriously. "It keeps me focused."

Jesus thought about that. Focused on what? He didn't think that Sriracha was lazy, but he'd never seen him do anything except smoke cigarettes and play video games. He never started his homework until time had almost run out.

Sriracha eyed Jesus.

"And what do *you* do to stay on the mark?" he asked.

"Right now, I'm reading the New Testament. It helps center me. Especially the four Gospels."

Sriracha gazed at his brother.

"Do you know the work of Marc Chagall?" he asked him.

Jesus nodded his head.

"He was a great artist and did some of the best portraits of the crucified Jesus that I have ever seen."

Sriracha was stunned. He never really talked to Jesus about *anything*. Now all of a sudden, he not only understood Jesus's fascination with the divine, but they shared a mutual fascination for the artist he admired.

"Mom's getting me a book about Chagall's work," he told Jesus. "You can borrow it if you want."

Jesus nodded and smiled happily.

Mili smiled and Mardie had to hold her hand over her mouth to keep from laughing.

Sriracha was a relaxed apparent ne'er-do-well whom she loved. Jesus was brilliant,

knowledgeable, and somewhat of a prig. The fun and poignant exchange she had just witnessed between them surprised and amused her. Oil and water mixing for a sublime nanosecond.

Mardie spoke up and asked Sriracha a question.

"Dear boy," she began. "Your mother tells me that you are seriously considering a career as a graphic novelist."

"It's true, Aunt Mardie," he replied. "I don't want any more history. Or English. And no more math or science. But I *do* want more art. Drawing. Inking. Coloring. Writing. Graphic novels require all of those."

"Awesome," Mardie said. "I don't think I've ever read a graphic novel."

"I have them brought down from Earth by the same devils who bring me video games. Those guys, by the way, think graphic novels are just expensive comic books, but they are more than that. They do use sequential art, but they have serious stories to tell."

"A little like illustrated books?" Mardie asked.

"Yes, but not with just a few color plates. Graphic novels are *filled* with art and accompanying text that explain and enhance the visual experience."

Mili was silently observing the interchange between Sriracha and Mardie. She was thrilled at his enthusiasm. She remained silent and watched the conversation continue.

"So, what topic have you selected for your first graphic novel?" Mardie asked.

"Well, that's a long time away," Sriracha answered modestly. "First, I have to become a good artist—*a consistently good artist*—before getting started on any stories. A graphic novel has hundreds of drawings and they have to be perfect." Sriracha spread his hands wide as if to show it was anyone's guess how long it would take him to be able to draw quality panels for a graphic novel.

"All right," Mardie said. "Though I don't think it will take you very long. Your father and mother are probably the smartest people anywhere in Heaven, Hell, *or* Earth. And *you* are just as smart as they are. You just have to be confident and let your talent shine."

Sriracha actually blushed.

"Thank you, Aunt Mardie," he replied. "I know that you are a great writer, so you're in that same gene pool, too."

"Swimming in the deep end with my nephews and niece," Mardie teased and winked at Jesus, who was observing everything.

"You're including me?" Jesus asked thrilled.

"Look buddy, you're probably the smartest one of all," Mardie told him. "And I'll deny I said that if anyone in your family remembers I said it."

Jesus and everyone in the car laughed hard. Of course, Jesus hoped with all of his heart that it was true. He didn't want to be a graphic artist, but the idea of studying to be a scholar had tremendous appeal for him.

"So, Sriracha," Mardie went on. "What kind of stories do you think you will start off with when your art is ready to go?"

Sriracha looked at his mother and then at his aunt.

"I want to do graphic novels about Mom's cases in Hell. The ones you worked on together. The first one will be called *The Wickett Sisters in Hell*.

"Cool," Mardie purred. The kid knew how to pitch a book.

"Not to be au contraire," Mili spoke up, "but everyone down here already knows all of those stories."

"I'm not going to be selling them *down here*," Sriracha answered. "I am going to have them published and distributed on Earth by a business that Dad bought shares in for me a long time ago."

"And which one would that be?" Mili asked him.

"IngramSpark," Sriracha responded. "*Spark*. Get it?"

Amused, Mili laughed and Mardie roared. There was more joy and laughter all the way to the kibbutz. It allowed Mili to briefly forget the words she'd heard way too many times that day. Gabriel is dead.

CHAPTER THREE

It's terrible, terrible news," David Ben-Gurion said as he and Mili discussed Gabriel's death. He shook his head over and over. "News that can hardly be believed."

Mili was sitting with David and Paula Ben-Gurion in their kibbutz apartment sharing afternoon tea. Mili's children had disbursed in search of their friends. And Mardie had gone off to visit Moshe Dayan.

"Have you heard anything at all from your husband?" David asked.

"Not a word," Mili told him. "He decided to travel to Heaven early this morning to see for himself what was going on. When did you hear that Gabriel had died?"

"We've known since before dawn," Ben-Gurion replied. "Demons told our drivers as they unloaded produce trucks in New Babylon."

"What did they know about Gabriel's death?"

"No one had any details, but everyone agreed that he had been murdered."

Mili shook her head yet again.

"Impossible," she whispered.

"No, dear," Paula said looking sad. "Apparently not impossible at all."

"Horrible thought though," her husband commented. "Everyone knows that heavenly beings can die—from Jehovah to the lowliest angels—but it occurs so rarely that it is easy to forget its truth and power. I've heard of demons down here succumbing or disappearing, but I never witnessed it. You, on the other hand, Milicent, you have seen dead angels before, have you not?"

"I have. They die just like humans. But unlike hellions, Jehovah cannot—or will not—restore them."

"That's a bit puzzling," Paula said.

"Did you ever happen to ask Lucifer about that?" her husband followed up.

"No," Mili answered. "I never thought about it to be honest."

"It's odd," Ben-Gurion said. "Humans are sainted or damned for eternity. But fallen angels—the heavenly beings who once surrounded God's throne—die and decay." David's face looked puzzled. "Why would Jehovah do that?"

"I am what I am," Paula quoted Jehovah as if to answer for him. "And I will be what I will be."

"Ain't it the truth?" her husband sighed. "God was oddly honest in that confession, wasn't he?"

"Yes," Mili remarked. "Though I personally think it was mostly a smart aleck remark tossed off at Moses who kept pressing him for a divine name that the Egyptian pharaoh would acknowledge."

Ben-Gurion sniffed and tossed his head.

"Egyptians."

Paula shook a finger at her husband.

"Let's not go there."

Mili smiled. She liked Paula. Mrs. Ben-Gurion had fearlessly ridden the tornado she'd married for a lot of decades. David knew her strength and her love and he cherished her. David folded his arms over his chest and kept his thoughts about Egyptians to himself.

"I am just stunned," Mili continued, "that everyone seems to believe that Gabriel was murdered."

"In Heaven!" David responded. "Have you heard that?"

"Yes, I did hear that," Mili said. "Mardie told me that's what the TV news is reporting."

Ben-Gurion bowed his head and stared at his hands.

"And how will this affect everyone?" Paula asked softly.

Ben-Gurion raised his head and glanced at Paula. Then he looked at Mili.

"TBD," he said. "To be determined."

✳ ✳ ✳

Despite the dark shadows seeming to beset Hell over the shocking death of Archangel Gabriel, Mili and her family had a wonderful dinner together at the kibbutz. The dining room was full of families and Little Mardie was so happy to see her mother and brothers that she kept hugging them every chance she got.

Her little brother Jesus gave as good as he got, hugging his sister tightly. Sriracha accepted Little Mardie's hugs dutifully, but Mili and Mardie reveled in her warmth and love. Little Mardie even made sure that David and Paula Ben-Gurion got hugs, and she was pleased that Moshe Dayan stopped by their table to say hello and collect a hug.

Mardie watched Little Mardie's cheery glow and listened to her happy banter. Arie sat next to her content and dignified, enjoying his girlfriend's loving time with her family. His own family lived on the kibbutz and he was planning to stay here and farm as they had done for twenty some years. Mardie looked from Little Mardie's face to Arie's face. And back again. Yep, she thought. They're sleeping together. Good on 'em. There was never enough love. Never enough shagging either, for that matter.

Gabriel is dead, Mardie thought again. She had never met the most famous angel of them all. But everyone who ever had dealings with him—including Mili and Lucifer—claimed that a sweeter, more tender, more considerate individual did not exist anywhere else in Creation. *And now he'd been murdered.* At least he had not been offed in Hell. She felt guilty thinking of her own self-interest, but she couldn't imagine what kind of repercussions would have been set off if the Archangel had been killed down here.

After dinner all of the children left to join friends. Many of them had known Little Mardie, Sriracha, and Jesus all of their lives. Mili invited the Ben-Gurions over for coffee and served homebrewed Starbucks along with a dozen of the little cake pops that the outlet sold. Paula declined a pop. David ate two. Mili finished off the other ten throughout the evening's conversation. She didn't feel embarrassed in the least. They were only a mouthful each, for God's sake.

Late in the visit Lucifer called Mili on her mobile phone.

"Hello, love," she answered. "Are you back?"

"Yes," he said. "Just."

Lucifer's face looked both careworn and angry on the phone screen.

"Are you okay?" she asked.

"No," he said sullenly. "Things are a mess in Heaven, and even though I spent a lot of time asking questions, I got very little information."

"I'm at the kibbutz with the kids," Mili told him. "David and Paula are visiting. We've hardly talked about anything else except poor Gabriel. May I put you on speaker phone?"

"That would be fine," Satan answered without enthusiasm.

Mili plugged the iPhone into Little Mardie's iPad on the coffee table and switched to speaker phone. Now everyone in Mili's living room could see and hear the Devil.

"Hello, everyone," Lucifer said.

Paula nodded. David gave a little wave. Mili just waited.

"It's pure chaos up in Heaven," Satan began. "The saints are wandering around the streets glum and inconsolable. The skies are overcast as if Jehovah has banned the sun from showing. I spoke to folks I know, from Job and Samuel to Maya Angelou and Stephen Hawking, and they all agreed that while no one has made an official announcement yet, word has spread everywhere that Gabriel is dead.

"I went over to the temple area thinking that perhaps some of the high-ranking angels might have some information. I found Raphael in the porticos around the courtyard meeting with a group of Thrones and Dominions. He was explaining what was known about Gabriel's death. Despite his great size—he's almost seven feet tall—he looked stooped. His chestnut hair was pulled back in a ponytail and his face was weary and tired. I waited until he was finished, at which point, he kindly walked over to me and put his hand on my shoulder.

"'Hello, Lucifer,' Raphael said quietly to me. 'Has word already reached the nether world that one of our brothers has died?'

"I answered yes and thanked him for referring to Gabriel as one of *our* brothers, and he smiled.

"'You are ever the Archangel,' he told me. 'And you will always be my brother.'

"I bowed my head, humbled at his kind words.

"Raphael continued, 'And after endless ages there are now only three of us. Gabriel is dead.'"

He spoke softly, and while he did not cry, there was passion and sorrow in his voice.

"I asked if anyone knew what happened to him.

"Raphael replied, 'No, but he was discovered here in the temple courtyard—'

"Raphael pointed at the colossal plaza in front of the gleaming marble temple, the home of God, with marble pillars on the front and massive doors made of solid gold.

"'Gabriel was sprawled out on his back, dead,' Raphael continued to convey to me. Two Powers found him early in the morning while they were sweeping and washing the courtyard. They ran to the doors of the temple where Raphael stood guarding the entrance and told him the horror they had discovered. Raphael didn't really believe them. 'The possibility of Gabriel stretched out dead in the courtyard wouldn't penetrate my mind,' he told me.

"Then I saw his body lying prone on the great granite floor of the courtyard. The reality of Gabriel's death hit me as powerfully as an oxen's kick to my stomach. He was lying on his back dressed in a white robe. His feet were bare and his golden hair was spread out beneath his head. His blue eyes were staring lifeless at the sky. There was no breath. No life. No Gabriel.

"I noticed a hole—perhaps three inches in diameter—drilled into his upper chest. It was coated with a thick carbon residue. As though Gabriel's chest had been both blasted *and* cauterized by a tremendous flash of light and heat. And his heart was gone. It had been destroyed by the fiery blast. Vaporized by a power that very few angels in Heaven possess."

Lucifer fell silent. David and Paula Ben-Gurion sat in shock, holding hands on the sofa, and trying to somehow absorb the tale that the Devil had spun. But it was not a tale. It was a true story of murder and assassination. The brutal murder of one of Heaven's own. Jehovah's Archangel had been brutally slain by a lightning bolt to the heart. Right in front of God's own house.

Mili spoke up at last.

"What was the disposition of the body?" she asked.

"Jehovah ordered it placed inside the temple. He did not talk to Raphael. Four burly Principalities brought a wooden pallet and carried Gabriel's body into God's home. Raphael didn't know any more than that, and when I asked him specifically if there were any murder suspects, he just shook his head.

"I had been wondering all along if Archangel Michael was involved," Lucifer confessed. "He is made of stuff that absorbs and feeds on suffering and death. On the rare occasion he visits Hell, all the demons disappear as though they've fled to the remotest corners of perdition.

"Then I began to think that perhaps Jehovah himself might be the executioner. But what in the world could Gabriel possibly have done to offend the Almighty? I couldn't even imagine. God didn't kill me when he had the opportunity during the Great Revolt after I had made every effort to kill him. So, what unimaginable transgression could Gabriel have committed to warrant Jehovah's worst punishment?

"Raphael's plan when I left was to mobilize saints and angels to search for a renegade demon—or a human assassin—who had somehow entered Heaven and done his dirty business."

"Raphael didn't mention any suspects in Heaven?" Mili asked her husband.

"No," Lucifer replied. "Raphael cannot imagine that any angel or saint in Heaven would carry out an assassination inside the Pearly Gates."

"Fine," Mardie replied, her tone indicating that the Archangel's position was anything *but* fine. "Seems like only yesterday that Raphael would have been persuaded that *nothing* could happen to Archangels in Heaven."

Satan grimaced, but he had no comeback. He did not share his own opinion, which was the same as Raphael's. There simply was not a single angel in Heaven who would want to kill one of the Archangels. And what humans good enough to be sainted would harbor secret murderous thoughts or deeds? None. It was absolutely impossible. He looked at Mili again.

"Is it all right if I come to the kibbutz tonight?"

"Of course, darling," Mili told him. "Pfot is already here though."

"Don't bother him," Satan replied. "I'll grab my Harley and be there in half an hour."

The iPad screen went black.

Mili sank back in her chair. She hated it when Lucifer rode his motorcycle at night. He rode fast and he refused to wear a helmet. Mili closed her eyes and fought down her rising panic. This was not the time—if ever there was—for *her* Archangel to die.

CHAPTER FOUR

Lucifer arrived at the kibbutz after midnight. He looked like a wreck. It was one of the few times Mili had seen him victimized by the elements. His frowning face was streaked with grime. His ponytail was blown into a wedge of blond waves shooting out from his shoulders. He wore jeans, a white T-shirt, and a black leather motorcycle jacket.

Paula Ben-Gurion had gone home, but David had stayed to welcome Lucifer back to the kibbutz. He and Mili had been drinking coffee like it was decaffeinated, which it was not. Thus, they were both wired for endless dialogue and just waiting for Lucifer to join in.

Mili went to the door when the Devil opened it. She stared at him, trying to hide her amusement at his wind tunnel appearance. Mili hugged her husband hard. He embraced her back and kissed her on the forehead, grateful that she remained the most important constant in his life. Lucifer nodded at David who nodded back.

"Coffee?" Mili asked Lucifer.

"Shower," he replied. "*Then* coffee." He gazed back at Ben-Gurion. "I'm glad you are here, David. I've never had a day like today. Never.

If you are willing to listen, I would love to have your reactions and your counsel."

"Of course," Ben-Gurion answered. "I waited hoping that you would feel like sharing."

"Shower," Satan repeated and walked upstairs to the master bedroom. Halfway up he turned and looked back at Mili. "Honey," he said. "I know it's late, but I think Mardie should join us. I earnestly believe that the Wickett sisters are going to be called on to find out who killed Gabriel."

Lucifer turned away and climbed the rest of the stairs. Mili looked at David with wonder and fear on her face. He nodded, seeing how profoundly Lucifer's surprise announcement had disturbed her.

"Whatever happens," he told her, "you and Mardie will be magnificent."

Mili sat down on an overstuffed chair across the coffee table from David. He sat on a large brown leather sofa, balancing his coffee mug on his knee.

"I've been in Heaven before," Mili told him. "I met Gabriel, too. Did you know any of that?"

Ben-Gurion shook his head no.

"I was not aware of either one of those things," he said. "And just for the record, I never experienced being in Heaven *or* meeting Gabriel."

"I woke up in Heaven after I died," Mili shared. "I was resting on the most comfortable bed I had ever been on in a lovely bedroom done in bright Caribbean island colors and furnished with white wicker furniture. There were picture windows revealing cloudless skies and a pristine ocean beach that stretched as far as I could see. I learned I was at a hotel designated for new arrivals. Over the next few days there were introductory sessions to life in Heaven given by angels who also answered any and all questions."

"So, you liked Heaven?" David asked.

"It was quietly splendid," Mili replied. "But for a person whose whole life had been my work—a homicide inspector at Scotland Yard—there was literally *nothing* for me to do. How lucky for me that after only a few days of reading and strolling around aimlessly I was told that Lucifer had requested my help to help track down a serial killer in Hell.

"That was the first time I met Gabriel. He delivered Jehovah's message asking me to assist the Devil. Lucifer had discovered a head-less corpse on his porch of all places. Then another. He was furious and distraught and had no idea how to find the perpetrator. The Archangel told me that God was hopeful that I would see my way clear to lending Satan a hand. He was so kind and so gracious. Such a lovely person."

"Did you think it strange that God was willing to help Lucifer?" Ben-Gurion asked.

"I didn't give it a moment's thought," Mili said. "All I could think was that I was being offered a case. An extraordinary case! I mean, a murder in Hell? Who'd ever heard of such a thing?"

"And here you are," David said. "All these years later."

"Who knew?" Mili said. "Jehovah revoked my sainthood in Heaven after I shot the wormhole traveler who'd been dumping bodies at Lucifer's house. All in all, though, being here beat the pants off of any life I could have led in Heaven. And never, ever would I have imagined that there would be a murder up there!"

Mili suddenly looked alarmed.

"Oh! I have to call Mardie."

Mili pulled her mobile phone out of her purse and called her sister. Mili glanced at her watch. It was already half past midnight.

Mardie answered. She looked wide awake and happy.

"Yeah, sis?" she asked.

"Sorry for calling at such a late hour," Mili apologized. "Lucifer just got home." She paused and then asked, "What are you doing up?"

"Moshe and I are watching Cecil B. De Mille's movie the *Ten Commandments*," she answered. "Whew, what a crazy flick. I haven't seen it since I was a kid. All I can remember from back then was Charlton Heston's bare chest when he did his slave-for-a-day thing," Mardie said. "The man was built like an Archangel. Speaking of which, is there any news?"

"Lu just returned from Heaven and has asked that you join us for a debrief. David Ben-Gurion is here, too."

"Can Moshe come?"

"I don't see why not," Mili answered.

"We'll see you in five."

The iPhone screen went dark. Mili set the phone down next to her purse and went to the kitchen counter to brew more coffee. She suspected that it was going to be a long night of talk. About violence. And murder. And mystery.

Did it get any better than that?

✳ ✳ ✳

Lucifer wore dark slacks and a white short-sleeved shirt. Mili had on red shorts and a cream blouse and was barefoot. She was sitting next to Satan on the sofa. Mardi had on navy shorts, a white tank top, and white sandals. She and Moshe were sitting in two overstuffed chairs across the coffee table. Ben-Gurion sat in another one next to them. Everyone had a mug of coffee. Mili had coffee, too, but she didn't really need it. She was plenty amped up already.

"Heaven is a mess," Lucifer said. "Everyone is wandering around in a daze. Crying. Moaning. Shaking their heads. Never saw the like of it. Apparently, the shock of losing Gabriel was bad enough, but dealing with the fact that the gracious and popular Archangel was brutally *murdered* has everyone completely unraveled."

The Devil paused. His face was pale and he was clearly upset himself.

"Raphael is circulating, trying to comfort people," Lucifer said. "There is no trace of Michael."

"On the run?" Mardie suggested rudely.

"Maybe," Lucifer admitted. "Or holed up in the temple with Jehovah. God has not made an appearance, nor communicated in any way since Gabriel's body was discovered."

"Which doesn't mean anything in and of itself," Mili offered. "When something goes wrong, God has a long history of making himself scarce," she said. "And we're not the only ones to think this. Medieval Catholic scholars coined a Latin term for it, *Deus absconditus*. The hidden God. Or more accurately, the *hiding* God. Absent when suffering abounds."

Ben-Gurion nodded solemnly.

"*That's* the God we Jews know about."

Moshe nodded as well.

"Jehovah himself even talks about how deliberate his absences are," Moshe said. "'In wrath I hid my face from thee.' It's a passage in the book of Isaiah."

"I've read that Bible verse," Mardie chimed in. "Didn't God say that after that he would show mercy?"

"He did," Ben-Gurion acknowledged. "We're all still waiting."

"The fact is," Lucifer said taking over the conversation again, "for *whatever* reason God is not showing his face in Heaven right now, it is adding panic to the general misery over Gabriel's death."

"Well," Mardie reacted, "*absconditus* or not, God is going to have to find out who killed his Archangel."

"Unless *he* did it," Mili dared to state.

"Oh, come on," Mardie rebutted. "He didn't kill Lucifer, and he was a much more deserving target than Gabriel."

Both Ben-Gurion and Dayan sat stunned at Mardie's remark. Mili stared at Mardie totally pissed off. The Devil's face was hurt and offended.

"Care to rephrase your words?" Mili said to Mardie, her tone furious.

"My bad," Mardie quickly confessed. "I'm not weighing Lucifer's merits against Gabriel's, and I'm sorry if it sounded like that. My point is that God *underreacts* regarding the deeds of his Archangels, not overreacts."

Mardie stopped talking for a moment. Then held her palm up as if she were a school crossing guard stopping traffic.

"And you know what?" she said. "I don't give a shit about God. It's not like he's ever been anyone's best friend. I think we should stop talking about that narcissist and start talking about how in the world Gabriel got killed. Presuming it wasn't his loving master, then who? And why?"

Mili nodded.

"Good point. Someone has murdered the Archangel. Which means that whoever they are, or wherever they are, we should be able to figure out who's guilty."

Lucifer's mobile phone chimed once. He had a new text. He pulled his iPhone out of his shirt pocket and read the text. Then he looked up.

"Mili," he said and looked at her. Then he gazed at her twin. "Mardie. It looks like you're not the only ones who think that a solution to Gabriel's murder is possible. Archangel Michael just texted me to ask if he and Raphael could talk to you both about coming to Heaven and investigating the circumstances surrounding Gabriel's death. They would like to come here and visit with you both. Now."

Mili stared at her husband.

Mardie answered for both of them.

"Yes," she said emphatically. "The Wickett sisters prowling around Heaven? Hell yes!"

"How long will it take them to get here?" Mili asked.

"I don't know," Lucifer answered. "I told them we were at the kibbutz and gave them its location in latitude and longitude."

"We have those down here?" Moshe asked amazed.

"Yes," the Devil answered. "Hell has been charted along with every inhabited planet in the universe. Raphael and Michael will likely travel through folded space using holes that we're probably not even aware of."

"And you've known both of these Archangels from the beginning, as it were?" Ben-Gurion asked.

"Ay," the Devil answered. "We were all created together very early after Elohim established their heavenly kingdom."

"Elohim?" Ben-Gurion went on. "As in the Hebrew Bible's plural for God, Elohim?"

"The very same," Satan told him. "A handful of Gods created the universe, the galaxies and the stars, the planets and all the livable places in them. Then they created angels, humans, and animals. Full house! When I was awakened, I was introduced to the other three Archangels—Gabriel, Raphael, and Michael—by a chatty and light-hearted member of the Elohim incarnated in an angel's form."

"How did that Elohim look?" Mardie asked fascinated.

"The God we met was tall, red-haired, and female. A goddess really. We didn't know it then, but *that* incarnation of Elohim was all about love and sex.

"The Archangels were given the job of commanding the legions of angels Elohim had created, and to look after the infinite numbers of worlds God had made. When things eventually went sour and I was ejected, only Gabriel and Raphael were left to watch over folks and places. Michael's role was narrowed to punishing those who offended Jehovah, the sole remaining God who had managed to bind and hide away the other divine manifestations of Elohim."

"Why didn't God just make more Archangels?" Ben-Gurion asked.

"I don't know," Lucifer replied. "Once the angels and Archangels were created, none was ever added to those numbers, despite millions of so-called rebel angels being slaughtered outright before the survivors found refuge down here in Hell."

"Angels don't reproduce?" Moshe asked.

"Archangels and angels are usually male. The only females are found in the lower ranks of angels—Seraphim, Cherubim, Principalities, and Powers—*and* among fairies, sprites, and pixies. However, male angels soon found out that *human* females could be seduced and impregnated. The resulting offspring were giants. Some of them are even mentioned in the Bible. Goliath the Philistine for instance."

"Then angels must possess DNA that is compatible with human genomes," Ben-Gurion declared.

"Yes," Lucifer said. "But like the offspring from many other animals that cross species to produce hybrid offspring, angelic progeny were not only mostly male, they were all infertile."

"Goliath, too?" Mardie asked.

"For sure," Satan said. "Didn't matter in his case though. He was big, gay, and proud."

"I'm surprised more angels aren't gay," Mardie commented. "They're so beautiful."

"Who says they're not?" Lucifer responded and left it at that.

"Getting back to the DNA thing," Mili spoke up, "let me ask the question as to whether or not Gabriel might be recreated? Given a new heavenly body as are the saints when they arrive in Heaven."

"Since God alone administers the replicant process, only he would know and/or decide if an Archangel could or should be recreated," Satan told her.

"Well, all that does is take us back to wondering if God killed Gabriel himself," Mardie remarked.

"He didn't," a voice uttered. "Or I wouldn't be coming down here to talk to Hell's most famous detectives, Mili and Mardie Wickett."

Suddenly a giant man materialized in Lucifer and Mili's kibbutz living room. Standing six and a half feet tall, he was a smashingly handsome man with blue eyes, freckles, and copper-colored hair done in cornrow braids that fell down to his shoulders. He was wearing a white robe and brown leather sandals.

"Raphael?" Mardie cried out. "Michael?"

"No," the figure replied. "You can call me Jesus!"

CHAPTER FIVE

Lucifer jumped up and shook Jesus's hand. Everyone else stood. One by one Satan introduced them.

"Jesus, this is my wife, Milicent Morningstar."

Jesus smiled kindly.

"Nee Wickett," he added. "Maybe history's greatest detective."

"My," Mili gasped. "But Heaven has everyone! Even Conan Doyle!"

Jesus smiled again.

"Doyle's character Sherlock Holmes is stupendous for sure," Jesus acknowledged. "But Doyle is just a writer and Holmes is only imaginary. *You* are the real thing." Jesus bowed respectfully. Then he looked over at Mardie.

"And Mardell Wickett, I presume, whom I am told is quite the detective as well. Though her criminal training was apparently mostly gained by hanging out with them."

Everyone laughed. Even Mardie.

"May I call you Mardie?" Jesus asked her.

"Oh, please," Mardie almost moaned. Who knew that Jesus of Nazareth looked like Jesus of Hollywood?

Jesus walked across the room to shake hands with David Ben-Gurion. He looked at David's chest and frowned.

"Aren't you supposed to be wearing a crucifix around your neck?"

David's eyebrows shot up and Jesus roared.

"Just yanking your chain, David. What an honor to meet you. You were a rock of courage and devotion to the Chosen People."

David blushed and shook Jesus's hand.

"Of course, there are rumors," Jesus continued, "that once in a while the Jews wish Jehovah would have chosen someone else." There was a twinkle in his eye. "Believe me, I can relate." Jesus held up his hands. Dark holes from the crucifixion nails were ancient wounds that had healed into torn flesh embedded with black blood.

Jesus gazed at Mili.

"I heard that when you first came to Heaven, the foot you'd lost to diabetes during your earthly life was not restored. You look all happy and healthy now."

Mili lifted her restored foot for all to see.

Jesus shook his head a few moments in disbelief. He looked at his hands and said, "Maybe I can get these fixed down here!"

No one knew whether to laugh or just die of embarrassment. Of all the Jesus's they'd seen in movies, or television, and Easter season church billboards, none of them were remotely like *this* Jesus.

He turned to Moshe Dayan and shook his hand. Then he reached out and touched his chest where his heart was. Moshe looked down at his hand and then into Jesus's eyes.

"Just offering a little help, my friend," Jesus told him.

Moshe frowned, puzzled.

"You'll figure it out," Jesus told him. "Bless you for your bravery and dedication to God's people. Now you need to move on to the place where you realize that every person of *every* faith is part of your family."

Jesus walked up to an open chair next to Mardie's.

"May I sit?" he asked.

"Please!" Mardie responded.

Mili spoke as Jesus sat.

"Would you like some tea? Or Starbucks coffee?"

"Coffee with lots of cream and sugar, please," Jesus told her. "Happy to say that I was one of the first coffee drinkers anywhere to visit a Starbucks. Way back in the 1970s. Went to church in Ballard up in north Seattle and worshipped with the happy charismatics at Dennis Bennett's church. Afterwards we recessed down the street to a new Starbucks outlet." Jesus looked at Ben-Gurion. "Howard is Jewish. Did you know that?" David nodded happily. "He likes to visit us in Heaven," Jesus went on. "Though he has to drink a lot of his own coffee up there just to stay awake."

"Ha!" Mardie said, at which everyone laughed. Being bored up in Heaven was not something anyone readily admitted, be they angels, saints, or God. Who was this Jesus Christ?

Mili brought Jesus's coffee. He thanked her and took a big drink. He looked surprised.

"Somehow I thought the coffee down here would be a lot hotter." Jesus grinned and looked person to person with the kindest look on his face.

"You're not who I would have expected," David said.

"So, you've read the Gospels?" Jesus asked.

"Yes," Ben-Gurion replied. "You came across in those stories a bit—"

"Of a prick?" Jesus interrupted.

David flushed.

"I was going to say a bit stiff," he clarified.

"That, too," Jesus graciously replied. "Remember that the Gospels were written decades after my life was over. By that time the Jews were getting blamed for everything that happened to me. My own Jewishness got taxidermied and my message for God's people got stuffed as well."

"Which was?" Moshe asked seriously.

"Feed the hungry. Clothe the naked. Visit the prisoners," Jesus replied simply. "If a person could show mercy to those people, he or she could love *anyone*. Piece of cake."

"Helping the helpless," Dayan said softly.

"Yes, but it's nothing new," Jesus told him. "Look up Exodus 22:22. 'You shall not mistreat any widow or fatherless child.'"

"Those are Jehovah's words?" Ben-Gurion asked, hardly believing what he had heard.

"Yes, they are," Jesus said. "Of course, he goes on to say, 'If you mistreat them my wrath will burn, and I will kill you with the sword.'"

"Now *those* are Jehovah's words," David responded not trying to hide his smirk. "'Be kind or I'll kill you,' saith the Lord."

Now Jesus grinned.

"Can you tell us what's happening right now in Heaven?" Moshe asked.

"I can, and that is why I asked Raphael and Michael if *I* could be the one who came down here to ask the Wickett sisters to help out."

Everyone sat quietly waiting for Jesus to share what he knew. He took a drink from his coffee and began.

"Gabriel's body was found early this morning by folks scrubbing the white granite
pavement stones of the courtyard in front of the temple. The temple is Jehovah's home, a
gleaming marble edifice on which Herod the Great's temple was based.

"Generally, Jehovah does not leave his home. The temple courtyard is busy with saints and angels who come to pray and meditate. And sometimes it is used by heavenly choirs singing praises to God. He enjoys those, though I've never seen him open the temple doors and actually *watch* a performance.

"Jehovah prefers to watch television. BBC mostly. He thinks British TV is the most dignified. He likes *Dr. Who, Sherlock Holmes,* and *Still Game*, a Scottish comedy about two pensioners taking on the establishment. The Almighty does not leave the temple. He claims that he can access any event anywhere in this or any other universe."

"But he missed Gabriel being murdered in front of his own house?"

"Yes," Jesus answered simply.

Mili thought about that a moment.

"I don't believe that we need to see Jehovah just yet," Mili told Jesus. "Not until the investigation requires it. I would like to see the Archangel's body, and if hasn't been moved to a morgue that should happen immediately."

"We don't have a formal morgue in Heaven," Jesus replied, "but we do have a hospital that has a small one. Truth be told, it's never been used. It is, however, stocked with standard autopsy tools. I helped with that. We want to be prepared for any emergency, I told the hospital administrator. Even dead bodies. The administrator was puzzled and I did not explain. But I thought that with God in residence, how could that not be a possibility?"

Jesus looked directly at Mili.

"Do you have lab facilities down here that can read and interpret DNA genomes?"

Mili nodded.

"Yes," she answered, "and it's been quite useful in helping me sort out bodies we often encounter in Hell that are missing heads, faces, and other body parts. File photographs can be inconclusive as to who is who, but the DNA profiles and matches nail everything."

"Can you tell me how the matching works?" Jesus asked.

"Of course," Mili replied. "The process of retrieving a sample of DNA and matching it against other samples requires an isolated strand of DNA, which is marked at thirteen different locations and then compared to the exact same locations on other samples. Any match that occurs very probably assures a physical relationship, and there is less than a one-in-a-billion chance of mistaken identification."

Jesus nodded.

"I would like to leave a personal DNA sample for examination by your lab, and I am formally requesting that you take DNA from Gabriel's body and perform a matching procedure with mine."

Mili nodded. How else could she respond? Was Jesus asking for a paternity test? Damn straight he was.

"What sample could I bring from Jehovah?" he asked. "I would like to have a matching procedure against his DNA as well."

"The lab personnel will use a swab to gather saliva from you," Mili replied, "and that will be used as your sample. As for Gabriel, I'll bring back something that will not show any denigration because of his death."

"Such as?" Jesus asked.

"A lock of hair most likely," Mili answered. "The same will work for Jehovah."

Jesus nodded.

"May I assume that all results will be kept private?" he asked.

"Absolutely," Mili assured him. "I will monitor the gene matching process myself and no one will know the results but me. And I will be the only one to discuss them with you."

"Do you need me to explain why I am requesting these personal tests?"

Mili shook her head.

"I don't think that's anybody's business but yours," she said.

Jesus smiled slowly.

"Might be my mother's business," he said. His eyes twinkled. "But then again, she already knows!"

✳ ✳ ✳

"Please brew another pot of coffee," Lucifer asked Mili. He looked at the others in his living room. Everyone nodded and lifted their coffee mugs. Jesus had gone, but no one else was leaving. Mili rose and started the coffee brewing. "Thanks, love," the Devil called after her.

"So, how are you, my friends?" he asked his guests. There was a general feeling of unbridled amazement in the group. Had they really and truly just witnessed a conversation with Jesus himself? Including his request to match his DNA with *two* possible fathers? That story wouldn't be getting into the Bible anytime soon.

"I have to admit that I found him remarkably charming," Mardie spoke up.

"Ay," Moshe agreed. "Down to Earth. Friendly. Straightforward and funny. Not anything like the Jesus I'd always heard about."

"Same here," Ben-Gurion said. "I always thought that Jesus was a snotty-nosed young bastard who had it in for Jews." He smiled hearing his own words. "Hardly, eh?"

"The chap you saw is the one I always see up in Heaven," Lucifer said. "Always greets me warmly. Asks about how things are. Is careful to give a heads up if the Old Man is in a mood. Which God almost always is when he knows that *I* have an appointment."

Mili made the rounds refilling everyone's coffee mugs with fresh coffee. They all took it black except her. She sat down and topped her coffee with cream and sugar.

"Quite a nice man, indeed," was her take. "But now I'm ten times as curious to know what kind of divinity is sitting all alone in the temple while all this shite is going on around him. Gabriel is dead. But does he care? I noticed that Jesus had nothing to report on that, and you'd think that he—of all people—would know how God was reacting to the tragedy. Do you suppose he hasn't talked to him yet?"

"Very likely he hasn't," Lucifer responded. "If anyone would know how God is dealing with this tragedy it would indeed be Jesus."

"At this point I'd be willing to settle for just knowing what *Deus Hidingawayfromus* even looks like," Mardie piped up.

Both David and Moshe raised their hands as though seconding Mardie's suggestion.

"Actually, I can help out with that," Satan told them. "I've seen him enough times." The Devil picked up his coffee and drank it as he talked.

"God's appearance is not all that impressive. He chooses to occupy the form of a shorter man, maybe five foot seven or eight. It's quite a contrast to the Archangels who tower from six and a half feet tall—Jesus's height by the way—to almost eight feet tall like Michael. Jehovah is barrel-chested, with long, wavy black hair that flows down his back. He wears white robes exclusively and plain leather sandals. He has shapely feet and fine hands.

"His face is handsome with even features, but his appearance tends to change depending on which television show or movie he's been viewing. He looked like James Mason for a long time after he watched *Lolita*. Then he favored George Clooney while he binge-watched the Oceans movies. Right now, he looks a lot like Benedict Cumberbatch. Big surprise since he watches *Sherlock*, eh? At any rate, he likes to be seen as a good-looking man.

"The one way in which he truly *is* exceptional *and* godlike—is his voice. It is very low—bass to the nth degree—and he enunciates very slowly. It sounds like a river of words flowing together. Think of George Beverly Shea singing at a Billy Graham crusade, only slurring his words as though under the influence. It is very unusual to hear. And to be honest, quite unnerving. Which pleases Jehovah. One caveat if you will," Lucifer said and held up a hand. "He may speak differently to other people than how he speaks to me. What I've described is what *I* encounter when I make an appearance before him."

"I think that's the voice he favors," Mili spoke up. "Remember when the Gospels describe Jesus's baptism and claim that God spoke from the heavens saying, 'This my beloved son, in whom I am well-pleased.' His voice was so low and so sonorous that most eyewitnesses denied that it was a voice at all, claiming instead that it was a peal of rolling thunder. Yet it seems to be exactly the voice Jehovah uses when he talks to you."

Mili looked around the living room. Everyone was nodding their heads. She glanced at her husband. He was also nodding and gave her a thumbs up. Rolling thunder indeed. It had clearly been the basso profundo of the Almighty altering his voice to impress the bystanders. Mili picked up her coffee cup and enjoyed a big taste.

Jehovah had said *my* beloved son, Mili remembered. At least that's what the Biblical account had touted. Now with Jesus requesting DNA tests, God's proclamation might be affirmed or denied. She didn't know what to hope for. That Jesus's DNA would match that of the Most High? Or that of the Archangel Gabriel who had told Mary that she would bear a special child?

Contrary to her attempt to posture as a neutral observer facilitating Jesus's genome matches, Mili hoped that after all was said and done, it would be the wonderful Archangel who had indeed provided male DNA for Jesus's incarnation. Sad news to hear just now, however, she thought. Gabriel is dead.

CHAPTER SIX

I need to see Gabriel's body as soon as possible," Mili told Lucifer. They were having tea and toast at the kitchen table with Mardie who had stayed over. No one had gone to bed until almost dawn and that had allowed for only a few hours of sleep. But who could sleep? A visit from Jesus. Hearing Satan describe Jehovah for the first time in anyone's experience. And on top of everything else, Mili and Mardie had received an invitation to come to Heaven and investigate Archangel Gabriel's murder.

"I want to see the cadaver before there are putrification issues," Mili explained. Mardie blanched. The Devil stopped eating his toast and stared at her. Mili noticed. "Or isn't that a worry with dead Archangels?" she asked.

"Putrification?" he responded. "Are you asking if Gabriel is starting to decay?"

"In a word," Mili replied, "yes."

Satan responded.

"Jesus promised to have Gabriel's body moved to Heaven's hospital morgue. I am sure that Raphael made sure that the chillers were turned on so the corpse should be cooled and ready for your inspection. Are you planning an autopsy?"

Mili shook her head.

"Really no need if it's true that a lightning blast to the chest disintegrated his heart." Mili scowled at the thought. "Gabriel probably saw who murdered him. And he likely didn't expect that individual to shoot him in the chest. Who could have wielded that kind of destructive power?"

"Some high-ranking angels possess a blast that powerful," Satan answered. "And, of course, so do the Archangels. If it wasn't done by one of them, it leaves only one other suspect, and *he's* the one who invited you and Mili to investigate."

Mardie ignored Lucifer's inuendo as she had before when he tried to throw suspicion on the Almighty.

"My next question is: how do we get to Heaven?"

"We'll use the wormhole I take when I appear before Jehovah," the Devil answered. "It's back at our New Babylon townhouse. Why don't you and Mardie head into town and use it? I'll stay here and keep an eye on the kids. The opening is in the kitchen, on the left side of the back door. It will put you in Heaven right at the temple's front entrance. Raphael will likely be there to greet you. He usually keeps a twenty-four-hour presence at that door."

"Guarding God?" Mardie asked.

"*Honoring* God," Lucifer corrected, countering Mardie's insult.

"Honoring him by keeping him alive?" Mardie pressed him. Satan frowned. "And are all the Archangels guarding the front door when *you* show up?"

✳ ✳ ✳

It went down exactly the way Lucifer said it would. Mili and Mardie stepped out of the wormhole and appeared at the foot of the temple. It gleamed white-and-gold beneath the overhead sun, blinding anyone who dared to look directly at it. Mili and Mardie walked up to the front of the temple's gigantic golden doors and Archangel Raphael welcomed them as they approached.

Despite his great size—more than seven feet tall—Raphael slumped, his shoulders rounded and hunched forward. His chestnut hair was pulled back in a ponytail and he looked weary and sad. He had a ruddy handsome face, but his good looks were marred by a deep frown. It was not their arrival that burdened the Archangel. It was everything else. Gabriel was dead. God was hiding. Heaven was panicking. He walked up to Mili and Mardie.

"Welcome," he said kindly. "I am Raphael."

Mili extended her hand.

"I am Milicent Morningstar."

Raphael shook her hand firmly. He smiled kindly.

Mili smiled back and introduced her sister.

"Raphael, this is my twin sister Mardie Wickett."

"It's an honor to meet you," Mardie said in awe. She stepped forward and reached up to shake Raphael's hand.

"Thank you," the Archangel replied. "But the honor is mine. Everyone here knows about the famous adventures of the Wickett sisters in Hell." He winked, which surprised both Mili and Mardie. "You have quite an avid group of followers in Heaven. And since your investigations stop evil and restore righteousness that makes your activities not only acceptable in Heaven, but a real joy to follow for both angels and saints alike. There's even talk about putting on dramatic reenactments of your cases."

Both Mili and Mardie burst out laughing. Raphael smiled, slightly embarrassed, not having any idea what he'd said to elicit their response.

"Forgive us," Mili quickly apologized. "We have our own reenactments in Hell. But they're Bible stories! And we *love* them. Having Wickett sister reenactments sounds hilarious."

Raphael grinned with relief and then laughed when he realized how funny his happy bit of news must have sounded to Mili and Mardie. Then he refocused on the sad business at hand.

STEPHEN HOUSER

"Thank you so much for coming. I am not authorized to take you to Jehovah yet, but I will—with your permission—take you to the hospital morgue. Gabriel's body was moved there several hours ago."

"Do I recall correctly that Gabriel's body was found near where we are standing now?" Mili asked.

Raphael nodded and walked a few steps closer to the temple doors.

"Right here," he said. "He was coming to replace me on guard duty and was apparently killed on his way. His body was found by courtyard cleaning folk."

Mili knelt and carefully inspected the huge granite tiles. Not a spot of blood. Not a dot of flesh. No carbon residue from the wound. No sign of any kind to mark the death of an Archangel. She stood up and looked at Raphael. He and Michael were the only remaining Archangels in Heaven. A verse from an old nursery rhyme suddenly jumped into her head. *There were two. And then there was one.*

Mili furrowed her brow. Where did that come from? Was it a warning that with Lucifer disgraced and Gabriel deceased, another of the last two Archangels was in jeopardy of being "taken out" as well? Maybe. Maybe not. How would she ever know all the possibilities up here in Heaven? This was not Hell. This was the *opposite* of Hell. She had to find a colleague up here. Someone to work with her and Mardie in Heaven.

Bloody good idea she decided with genuine excitement. The greatest detective minds in the history of the universe were here in Heaven. Not to mention the best of the best crime mystery writers. Somewhere in Heaven was the very person who'd help crack this case. Now she only had to find him. Or her.

✳ ✳ ✳

Mili wore a white laboratory smock, a surgeon's mask, and yellow latex gloves. She was alone in the hospital morgue with Gabriel's body. Mardie had refused to come along. She was sitting in the hospital lobby waiting.

The morgue was a small room with just enough space for a single metal gurney. There was a drain in the floor beneath it, a sink on the wall, and a cabinet with autopsy tools and supplies. The Archangel lay on his back on the cart taking up virtually its entire length with his seven-foot corpse. He was naked except for a folded white towel covering his hips and male parts. His eyes were closed and his face was expressionless.

Mardie looked at the deceased Archangel. His over-the-shoulder blond hair was tangled and his skin had turned lead-gray. He had a muscular body with no evidence of fat anywhere on his frame. There were no moles, or age spots, or skin tags. No circles or bags under his eyes. No lines or wrinkles on his beautiful face. Did Gabriel know how handsome he was? Likely not. He was always so humble and unassuming.

She looked at his feet. He had four toes on each foot and long narrow planter surfaces that would have made him a great long-distance runner. Did he run? Men in the Old Testament routinely walked or ran thirty miles a day if required. The invincible Roman army legionnaires could march twenty miles a day, build a fenced camp every night, and do it all on bread and beer.

Gabriel had large beautiful hands. Exactly like David's in Michelangelo's giant sculpture of the ancient warrior. In fact, Mili suddenly realized, the sculptor's fourteen-foot-tall marble David was *not* David at all, it was Gabriel. The statue was twice the Archangel's height, but it was clearly a perfect stone copy of his torso, his chest, his face, and his hands. What was the story behind that, Mili wondered?

Mili bent over and looked at the wound in Gabriel's chest. It was a miniature crater. Three inches wide and twice as deep. The flesh was gone. The sternum was gone. The heart was gone. She stared inside the cavity. The flesh had been cauterized around the hole coating the sides of the wound with a black carbon crust from the blast and its heat.

She had never seen an injury like this. Whatever weapon or super-natural force had been used on Gabriel had disintegrated, dissolved, and destroyed both flesh and bone, leaving an empty cavity in his chest. She had witnessed bodies killed by lightning strikes—flesh tattooed with a spider web of heat damage smelling like a blue plate special at a local pub—but this injury required a weapon the likes of which she could not identify.

Unless the devastation had indeed been created by a weapon that the ancient gods had reputedly used. *Lightning bolts.* Wielded by Greek gods like Poseidon. Semite divinities like Moloch. Zoroastrian deities like Ahura Mazda. The never-to-be forgotten Hindu goddess Kali. And, of course, Jehovah, God of the Jews.

Mili walked over to an old-fashioned rotary wall phone and put the receiver to her ear. She dialed 0 for the hospital operator.

"This is Milicent Wickett," she said when her call was answered. "I'm working in the hospital morgue with Jehovah's permission. I am looking for the services of a police surgeon with Scotland Yard autopsy experience." Mili had used such professionals down in Hell and her hope was that one or more of them up here would be associated with Heaven's hospital. The operator said there was only one doctor in the hospital at the moment. She'd transfer Mili's call to him.

"Schweitzer here," the physician answered.

"Doctor Schweitzer, my name is Milicent Morningstar. I have been asked by Jehovah to investigate the circumstances surrounding Archangel Gabriel's death."

"Welcome, Mrs. Morningstar," the doctor answered. "I am aware of your task and I am willing to help in any way that I can."

"Do you have a Scotland Yard background?"

"No, I'm afraid not. But I was a private physician who performed work on a multitude of diseases and injuries. I saw it all in my forty years in the clinic."

"I am in need of specific surgery on a wound on Gabriel's cadaver," Mili responded. "Can you free yourself to help me for a few minutes?"

"No problem," the doctor replied immediately. "I am finishing rounds—such as they are with no patients—and I can meet you in two minutes."

"Thank you, Dr. Schweitzer," Mili told him.

"It will be my first time in the morgue, you know," he said and hung up.

Mili appreciated his willingness to assist her. She knew the name Schweitzer. Could it be the world-famous doctor who had dedicated his life to working with Africa's poor? The good doctor arrived promptly. He was tall and thin. He had a tanned face and sported a large white walrus moustache. And a thick mane of white hair. She'd seen his picture printed over and over in the *London Times* as a child. It was indeed *the* Albert Schweitzer, and he was still helping people.

The doctor extended his hand.

"Albert Schweitzer," he said and shook Mili's hand. He put on a lab coat and latex gloves, chatting away the whole time as he did. Once his face mask went on, however, he stopped talking and approached Gabriel's cadaver.

Mili stood next to him and pointed at the Archangel's injury. She told Dr. Schweitzer that she wanted to observe the tissue at the bottom of the wound.

"May I cut into it?" Schweitzer asked.

"No one in here is going to mind," Mili answered.

Dr. Schweitzer gave a little laugh. A sort of professional chortle to acknowledge Mili's macabre humor. He picked up a scalpel and a tweezers from the tray of autopsy tools and pulled a small stack of clean white towels closer. Then he bent over Gabriel's open wound and started.

He cut four incisions on the inside of the injury and used the tweezers to pull away the burned skin and charred muscle. Several of the Archangel's spinal vertebrae were exposed. Dr. Schweitzer picked up a dental pick and proceeded to pick quite forcefully at one of them.

51

The morgue phone rang. Mili started at the sound. Dr. Schweitzer stopped and stared at her. Mili held her hand up signaling the surgeon to hold a moment. She walked over and answered the phone.

"Yes?"

"Mili, it's Lucifer. I'm in the hospital lobby. Mardie and Raphael are here, too. All of us—and you—have been summoned to an audience with Jehovah."

"I'm just wrapping up here. Can I meet you in five minutes?"

"You can meet me in *thirty* seconds," Lucifer shot back. "Whatever you're doing it can wait."

Mili hung up and told Dr, Schweitzer that she had to leave on an urgent errand, but would return as soon as she could to review his observations. The doctor nodded politely and went back to picking at Gabriel's backbone. Mili stripped off her gloves and mask. She tossed them in a plastic bin, recycled her lab coat in a wicker hamper, and left the morgue.

Lucifer waved as she approached and then motioned for her to move faster.

"What in Hell?" she complained when she reached him.

"No," The Devil corrected her irritably. "It's *who* in Heaven. God is waiting for us. Now!"

CHAPTER SEVEN

Raphael led Mili, Mardie, and Lucifer across the great courtyard to the front of the temple, God's home. Two twenty-foot-high golden doors marked its entrance. Raphael asked the group to pause while he went over some basic protocols.

"Lucifer knows the rules," he said. "You ladies, however," he nodded towards Mili and Mardie, "are first-time guests. You will be pleased to observe that Jehovah is down-to-Earth and informal. However, *don't* confuse that with a mistaken assumption that he desires familiarity.

"Jehovah requires and demands respect. He will also likely not invite you to sit, and it is best not to speak to him unless requested. He doesn't welcome comments. He does not like questions. You have been granted an audience because *he* has issues to discuss. These are not your issues. They are *his* issues.

"And should you feel an inclination to ask universal questions like 'What is the meaning of life?' or 'Do you answer prayers?' Don't. Doing so will likely result in Jehovah's request to have you immediately expelled by the Archangel on duty. Namely me."

Raphael smiled sweetly.

"Any questions anyone?" he asked. "*This* is the time to ask them."

"What kind of mood is Jehovah in?" the Devil asked.

"He's sad," Raphael said reflectively. "But irritated as well over the death of Gabriel. Contrary to anecdotal claims that the Almighty knows everything, he does not know who murdered his beloved Archangel. He is not happy about needing to look to Lucifer for help, but is consoled by the fact that the renowned Wickett sisters are willing to try and find the Archangel's killer."

Raphael swung open one of the golden doors and led the party inside. A long hall led to the interior. It was clad in marble walls and lighted by a peaked roof made of stained glass. The effect was subdued and beautiful.

Raphael led everyone to the chamber at the end. The Holy of Holies. The personal residence of Jehovah. The Lord God of all that was, is, and ever would be. There was an open doorway and Raphael entered. Lucifer nodded at Mili and Mardie. They followed Raphael. Satan went last.

The room was softly lit by old-fashioned multi-spout bronze lamps. They were filled with olive oil and lit by flaming wicks that protruded from holes in their tips. The room had a television screen so large it filled an entire wall, at least twenty feet wide and fifteen feet high. It was turned off. There was only one piece of furniture in the room. A large Greek-style recliner covered with large pillows.

Jehovah was stretched out on it, his hips snuggled into the pillows. He used his left arm to prop himself up to face his visitors. He was barefoot and wearing a long white robe, which covered his shoulders and extended down to the middle of his calves. Sleeves covered his arms and revealed his small, beautiful hands. Jehovah had long raven-black hair with purple highlights, and a large head, slightly out of proportion to his average-sized male body. He looked like Benedict Cumberbatch, though he was likely unaware that his visitors had been prepped by Lucifer to expect exactly that.

He also had a voice similar to the British actor's mellifluous voice, welcoming his visitors as they arrived.

"WELCOME MILICENT AND MARDELL WICKETT,"
Jehovah declared loudly.

Mili frowned, listening intently to what sounded like a greeting to Mardie and her. The words flowed into each other smoothly, the syllables gliding together in such a way that it was difficult to know when words started or ended. Wow. Rolling thunder, indeed, Mili thought.

"I can't understand a word you're saying," Mardie whined.

Both Raphael and Lucifer instantly cowered and Mili felt her stomach knot up. She stared at Mardie panic-stricken.

"DO YOU DARE TO ADDRESS THE KING OF THE UNIVERSE?" Jehovah roared.

Mardie nodded her head.

"Only because I can't understand you, your Mightiness," she told him.

With a truly disgusted expression on his face, Jehovah glared at Raphael as if this foolishness was his fault. Only then did he make an effort to be understood.

"Welcome Mardie Wickett," God said. **"I hope you are as talented as you are obstreperous."**

"I understood *that,*" Mardie replied.

"Ha!" Jehovah said and chuckled. He spoke in a normal voice now. "Welcome to you as well, Milicent Wickett. It is not often that Hell's residents are invited to Paradise." He glanced at Satan. "Lucifer visits periodically. But never without some issue to fix." Jehovah looked at the Devil again. "How are you, Lu?"

"No complaints," he replied tersely.

"You mean other than the fact that I am still alive and well?" Jehovah said without a hint of humor in his voice.

"No complaints at all," Lucifer replied, steering clear of God's rude remark.

"HA!" Jehovah blasted out and laughed loudly. "Just giving you some grief, Lu. I owe you my gratitude for encouraging your wife and sister-in-law to give me a hand on Gabriel's sad demise." Jehovah paused and appeared to meditate on the death of his beloved Archangel.

"I have searched the universe for any clue as to why someone would want to kill Gabriel. Forever the righteous angel, he was loyal, obedient, and selfless. A divine servant to be imitated. He also maintained cordial relations with weak, willful, and egoistic humanity. Legions of creatures always eager to express their ingratitude, selfishness, and angry complaints. I don't know how he did it. I personally steer totally clear of such sinners."

"Do you actually ever see anybody at all?" Mardie asked. "Bad *or* good?"

Jehovah stared at Mardie and scowled.

"Are you trying to provoke me again?" he asked, his voice rumbling ominously.

Mardie's face grew anxious. Mili and Lucifer stared at her, their own faces etched with worry. What was the point of antagonizing the Deity *in his own home?*

"Well, I think I might be, Lord," Mardie confessed. "I am doing so much to my own surprise, however, never having believed in you until I wound up in Hell. I guess I have a lot of old resentments about the earthly life you gave me and the utter and complete lack of interest you showed in my worthless shite of an existence."

Jehovah sat up straight and glared at Mardie. He was furious, but for whatever reason he mastered his rage and answered Mardie calmly.

"You made your *own* choices, Mardell Wickett," he spoke, his tone hard. "Who was I to interfere with those? Free will remember? And your trespasses are also your own. You allowed your father into your bed, then killed him for entering it."

"And you couldn't have saved me from all that?" Mardie cried.

"You didn't even acknowledge my existence, Mardell," God answered, raising his own voice. **"How hypocritical it is for you to criticize me now."**

Mardie went silent. She didn't like God, but she was hardly in a position to feel superior to the Divinity. They glared at each other for a moment. Then they called it a draw.

"There are many people who harbor ill feelings toward me, Mardell," Jehovah said. "It is to be expected considering the many disappointments people experience and then decide to blame on me. But Gabriel was different. He knew I was mercurial and complex, saving those I wished, and turning my face away from whomever I chose to hide. Gabriel, on the other hand, was always a loving being. He had no critics. He had no enemies. Yet he is gone. Murdered. Dead and carted to the morgue. **Find that person for me.**"

"Do you hear prayers?" Mardie asked.

Mili reached for Mardie's arm, stunned and upset that her sister couldn't keep her mouth shut.

"I hear every prayer uttered by everyone, Mardie Wickett. Jew, Christian, Muslim, Buddhist. I also hear the cries of agony and grief from agnostics and atheists. I even hear the stricken groans of animals in trouble or need."

"Animals?" Mardie replied surprised.

"Yes," God told her. "Only the other day a Nile crocodile cried out to me, 'My Creator, I am dying of starvation. Save me, Oh, my God!'"

"You heard the prayer of a crocodile?" Mardie asked in an astonished voice.

Jehovah nodded.

"I also heard the petition of a local Christian pastor who prayed for his safety and the safety of eight souls he had led into the Nile to be baptized."

"What happened?" she asked.

"The crocodile ate the pastor."

"You allowed that?" Mardie gasped.

"I didn't prevent it."

"My God…"

Jehovah smiled.

"Baptizing people in a river full of starving crocodiles, Mardie? The man was an idiot."

"But maybe he was full of faith?" she guessed.

"More like full of shit," Jehovah commented. "A lesson for you and everyone else. There are consequences for every action. *Every* action."

Mardie put her hands to her face and moaned out loud.

Jehovah smiled and motioned for her to stop.

"I'm just yanking your chain, Mardie," he said. "I had no idea what the crocodile was going to do. He did eat the pastor, though. The reverend is up here now. Blessed fool. And speaking of consequences for every action," he went on, "I want Gabriel's murderer found. A violent death was meted out to my faithful Archangel. He deserved no such thing. He was a pure creature. Untainted."

Mili was relieved that the conversation had turned again to the death of the Archangel. She stepped in immediately.

"Gabriel was killed by a fiery blast to his chest," she said. "I am not sure who in Heaven is capable of wielding that kind of blow."

Jehovah nodded and answered.

"A few angels have such firepower. An Archangel could wield a bolt to kill someone." Jehovah locked eyes with Mili. "And me. *I* could have killed him.

"I can drill a fatal bolt through anything," Jehovah went on. He stood up and extended his right hand toward the seat of the couch he had been sitting on. A cold blue laser-like bolt shot from his hand and cut through the recliner in an instant. The cut smoked, but the couch did not burn.

"Or I can conflagrate the whole thing with a mighty blast," Jehovah said, sending out a fiery stretch of shivering fire just like a flamethrower. The couch burst into flames and was consumed in a moment. Only a smattering of black ashes covered the white granite floor of the Holy of Holies.

"And, of course, I can combine those two heavenly bolts into something tailored to exactly kill an Archangel." A blast of fire maybe two inches thick shot from Jehovah's index finger directly at Lucifer's chest. With a flash of his hand, Raphael directed his own lightning bolt and deflected God's fire off its mark. Jehovah put his hand down. So did Raphael. Lucifer froze, speechless. Mardie was horrified and silent.

Not Mili. She spoke up, direct and professional, but with anger simmering beneath her words to Jehovah.

"Quit wasting my time," she lectured God. "Believe it or not, I have things to do in Hell. To come to your aid requires that you stop using my time for your stunts. We all know that you're the king of the universe. We all know that your Archangel Gabriel was murdered. Will you join me in making some kind of effort to find out who that murderer is instead of playing these childless games?"

Jehovah just stared at Mili. Mardie was sure he was going to raise his hand again and blast her one. But he did not. A thin smile appeared on his lips. He bowed his head in Mili's direction.

"To the point," he told her deliberately speaking loudly. **"I will help you in any way that I can to find the fiend who killed my Archangel Gabriel."**

"Thank you, Lord," Mili replied respectfully. "You can start by letting me return to the morgue where Dr. Schweitzer is concluding an examination of Gabriel's wound."

"GO!" Jehovah commanded. **"TELL AL HELLO FOR ME AND ASK HIM TO PLAY SOME BACH ON THE PIPE ORGAN FOR YOU SOME TIME."**

＊ ＊ ＊

"What an asshole!" Mardie muttered as she and the rest of Jehovah's audience walked out of the temple into the huge courtyard.

Raphael frowned.

59

Mardie noticed.

"I'm sorry," she told him. "But how can you stand that guy?"

"He is the Lord of all things," Raphael answered. "He is who he is. And he will be who he will be."

Mardie just shook her head and bit her tongue.

Lucifer stopped and extended his hand toward Raphael.

"Thank you, old friend," he said emotionally. "You saved my life."

Raphael shook the Devil's hand not really knowing what to say. Jehovah could have just as easily turned the fire on him for intercepting his blast at Satan.

"Yes, Raphael," Mili added. "I will never forget your brave act. Thank you for sparing my husband. For me and his three children."

The big Archangel blushed and led the party across the courtyard.

"Do you still wish to return to the hospital morgue?" he asked.

"Yes, please," Mili answered. "I want to see what Dr. Schweitzer has concluded regarding Gabriel's death blow."

Raphael nodded and led the way.

It had taken Albert Schweitzer longer to finish up than he expected. He had reached a long tweezer into the opening he'd made from Gabriel's wound and grasped something embedded in the Archangel's spine. He twisted until it came free. He walked over to the metal sink and washed the item under very hot water. Then he left it on the edge of the sink.

When Mili returned to the hospital morgue Dr. Schweitzer picked up the item he had extracted from Gabriel's vertebrae and asked Mili to hold out her hand. She did. The doctor laid the object on her palm. Mili stared at it in disbelief. It was the scratched and blunted slug of a spent lead bullet.

CHAPTER EIGHT

I want to leave," Mardie told Mili the moment she saw her. She stood and faced her twin. "I *hate* it here." Lucifer had waited with her. He stood up and came over.

"I understand," Mili replied. "Lu, is Pfot available?"

Lucifer shook his head.

"He's at the kibbutz right now. Remember? Watching the kids."

Mili looked at Mardie.

"I can take a taxi back to the kibbutz. Why don't you just come with me? Better to have some company when you're upset."

Mardie nodded.

"Anywhere but here. *I can't stand it!* And I'm not coming back. God is just plain creepy. And to think that he's in charge of everything makes me completely disgusted."

Mili looked at Satan.

"Can you come with us, too? We have a lot to talk about."

"I have to check in at the office," he replied. "But I promise I'll get out to the kibbutz tonight."

"Thank you, darling," Mili said, then stood on her toes and planted a long kiss on his lips.

"I'm not sure yet how much I despise Jehovah. But I do know how much I love you."

✳ ✳ ✳

By one o'clock, Mili and Mardie had returned to the Ben-Yehuda Kibbutz. A New Babylon taxi had dropped them off and disappeared. Mili called Moshe Dayan and the Ben-Gurions and invited them to afternoon tea and cakes. Moshe and David accepted happily. Paula was off quilting. By half two everyone was seated at Mili's kitchen table drinking Twinings tea and eating Fortnum & Mason Piccadilly biscuits. They had all three grown up on British sweets and they were a welcome afternoon treat.

Mardie was wearing white shorts and a red halter top. She was barefoot. Mili had on a pink blouse, taupe shorts, and natural-colored leather sandals. Both Moshe and Ben-Gurion had on black slacks, white short-sleeved shirts, white socks, and sandals. Mili had not yet told David and Moshe about her audience with Jehovah, but after seeing the frown on her face, neither man had great expectations. David finally spoke up.

"So, Mili, not the greatest experience, eh?" he asked.

Mili shook her head and responded.

"It was so bizarre my skin crawls just thinking about it," she answered. "Jehovah lives in a man cave in his copy of the Jerusalem temple. Or maybe his is the original and the Herodian one is a copy? I'm not sure how it works. Anyway, he reclines on a couch and the only other thing in the room is a giant telly. I mean *GIANT*. Like a twelve-hundred-inch screen."

"And he actually watches television shows?" Moshe asked stunned.

"Yes," Mili answered. "At least ones broadcast on BBC. Raphael says he likes *Sherlock Holmes* and *Dr. Who*. Oh, and *Still Game*. God is very off-putting. Like dealing with Donald Trump. He has a warped sense of humor and is a total megalomaniac. Yet he went tit-for-tat with Mardie's sarcasm as though it was just a bit of a merry exercise with a dafty."

Both Ben-Gurion and Dayan sat without moving. They were shocked beyond speech. It was the God of the universe Mili was describing, not some eccentric headmaster at a private school.

"I'm glad I don't live in Heaven," Mili said. "It's safe down here. Not up there. Jehovah demonstrated the kind of power that might have been used to shoot Gabriel. Without warning he fired a lightning bolt straight at Lucifer. If Archangel Raphael had not instantaneously intervened and warded off the blow with his own bolt of fire, Lucifer would be dead now."

No one spoke. What was there to say? That God is a lunatic? A misfit? Not to be trusted to run the very universe he created? The reality of God's alien and bizarre personality was like discovering that your estranged parent is not only someone who can't love you, but is, in fact, an immoral criminal who would just as soon kill you.

Moshe looked at Mili.

"Jehovah deliberately tried to strike Lucifer with a lightning bolt?" he asked horrified.

Mili nodded, still stunned at how she had almost lost her husband. Did God know that Raphael would intervene? Did he care? Probably not any more than he cared about Gabriel. What he really cared about was that one of his Archangels *had been taken from him*. And he would tear Heaven apart to find out who had done it.

"At the risk of failing to bash Jehovah," Ben-Gurion piped up. "I lived a very happy life on Earth and I am having an even better life in Hell. Who or what Jehovah is doesn't matter to me."

David looked directly at Mili.

"Having said that, I am kind of curious about whether you and Mardie made any progress on your case up in Heaven."

"Mardie and I did experience a strange twist in regards to that," Mili answered. "I examined Gabriel's cadaver, fairly sure that the fatal wound in his chest was delivered by some kind of bolt of fire to his chest. The flesh and bone had been disintegrated and a hole had been blasted all the way down to his spine.

"We were called away to visit with Jehovah, but a doctor from Heaven's only hospital continued in the morgue without me. He examined the wound and recovered a bullet lodged in the Archangel's spine."

Moshe narrowed his eyes waiting for more. David shook his head and scowled. Gabriel had been shot with a gun? In Paradise?

Mili went on.

"The Archangel was shot in the heart. Then his murderer went to the trouble of disguising the wound with a bolt that created the burned flesh. And why? Surely to fool Jehovah into thinking that only an angel had killed Gabriel, when, in fact, *anyone* in Heaven could have shot him to death with a gun.

"Lucifer is having ballistics run on the slug. It was small and definitely not ammunition from a larger and more powerful handgun like a Sig-Sauer or a Beretta. I didn't recognize it, but we might know as early as tonight what kind of gun it belonged to when Lucifer joins us here at the kibbutz."

"How, if I may ask," Moshe questioned, "did your husband handle the visit with Jehovah?"

"He was pretty subdued," Mili responded. "I think that he has had to deal with Jehovah so often that he just keeps his speech to a minimum and gets the hell out."

"And how did he react to being the target of Jehovah's lightning bolt?"

"He seemed to shrug it off. *I* was the one who got infuriated."

Moshe pursed his lips and thought about Mili's remarks. It reminded him of how both Hitler and Stalin had treated their generals. Pin medals on their chests and then shoot them. They were not alone. The Bible's King Saul was glad that young David had played the harp for him. Then he tried to kill him with a spear. Power corrupts. Absolute power means everybody around you better watch out.

"I was pretty surprised to hear that someone in Heaven has a gun," Mardie added, speaking up for the first time. "Fiery blasts suit that place. But *gunning down* an Archangel just didn't feel right. I asked Lucifer about that while we waited at the hospital for Mili. I was surprised to hear that there are more guns in Heaven than in Hell.

"It's a real effort to get a gun smuggled in down here," Mardie continued. "Several years ago, most members of the small fraternity of gun smugglers in Hell got shot down, bless the irony. One or two still operate in defiance of Lucifer's ban, but so far no one else has been targeted down here.

"Heaven on the other hand allows anyone to own any kind of gun. Pistols, rifles, semi-automatic weapons, arms for battle, hardware for armies. Lucifer thinks the reason for this is that until now no one had ever shot anyone else in Heaven. Which makes Gabriel's shooting death a terrible first. So terrible, in fact, that someone worked very hard to disguise that very distinction."

"We know that a bullet can be matched to the ordnance that fired it," Moshe reacted. "Is it possible that lightning bolts could be similarly unique? One-of-a-kind signatures that would make it possible to match them to specific owners?"

"I don't know," was Mili's take. "But the fact is that we are on more familiar ground
searching for a specific kind of gun based on the recovered slug and tracking down who
in Heaven owns one."

"Is there gun registration up there?" Ben-Gurion asked.

"That's a great question," Mili answered. "For now, I have to say again that I just don't know."

"Well, based on the Jehovah who I met today," Mardie spoke up, "I doubt very much that he cares who owns guns."

"He might once he finds out that Gabriel was killed by a gunshot," Moshe offered.

"You're probably right," Mili agreed. "However, he's not going to get that information from us just yet. We're going to keep our cards very close to our chests until we learn more about who owns guns in Heaven, and who might have wanted to hide the fact Gabriel was shot by disguising a bullet entry wound with angel fire."

Both David and Moshe nodded. They had kept many secrets about assassins that Israel's intelligence community—the mysterious and feared Mossad—had uncovered and used to track down foreign murderers who had been unwise enough to hurt Israeli citizens. They instinctively supported Mili's decision to keep God out of the loop while she investigated the Archangel's murder, allowing her to keep her investigation pure and her options open. Of course, if Mili found out who the murderer was, they still had friends in the Mossad who could eliminate that individual—even in Heaven—without anyone knowing it.

"So, what next?" Ben-Gurion asked Mili.

Mili perked up at the question.

"I need local intelligence," she said. "Someone who knows Heaven's turf. Someone who knows who's who and what they're up to inside the Pearly Gates. And maybe most important of all, someone who can investigate on par with the best."

"You're talking like you've already got somebody picked out," Mardie said.

Mili smiled slowly and contently.

"I do," she answered her sister. "Someone who should be thrilled to be recruited to help solve Heaven's first homicide." Mili paused. Mardie, David, and Moshe leaned forward in anticipation. "She was Britain's Lady Mallowan, DBE."

Everyone looked completely confused.

Mili smiled, then explained.

"She is the greatest crime mystery writer who ever lived. You know her as Agatha Christie."

* * *

Lucifer arrived at the kibbutz after dinner and after the departure of Mili's guests. She had had a chance to see all of their children earlier. She got kisses and hugs from Little Mardie, who then went off with Arie to a kibbutz screening of the film *Exodus*. Sriracha introduced her to the three chaps he currently ran around with. All of them were sweet goofy boys. Wild hair, unclipped fingernails, and dirty faces. Didn't those lads have mothers? Sriracha smoked like a furnace in a Minnesota winter, but *he* never looked unattended.

Jesus sat on her lap for a while even though he was already seven years old. The boy was born to be a love. He was temperamentally suited to grow up and become the scholar he hoped to be. But he was so much more. He had compassion. He visited the sick. He wanted everyone in Hell to be healthy and whole. Mili shook her head. He was more godlike than God.

Mili was reading an Agatha Christie mystery she'd borrowed from Moshe Dayan. He owned an English copy of *Death on the Nile* that had been a gift from Anwar Sadat. She herself had never read much of Christie, finding her drawing room crimes and proper characters a bit too upper crust for her. Yet why not? She was the wife of a rich and famous aristocratic archaeologist who had—among other exotic field experiences—helped Sir Leonard Wooley excavate Ur in Central Asia. Many of the great treasures they had unearthed now graced the British Museum.

Lucifer knocked and entered the apartment. He looked rather cheerful considering he'd almost lost his long and amazing life earlier today. He hugged and kissed Mili tenderly, then sat at the kitchen table and asked her to fix him a cup of coffee. She did, making one for herself as well.

"You look rather splendid considering the events we shared in Heaven today," she told him as she filled the coffeemaker with water. Lucifer was wearing chinos and a white Polo shirt. He had on tan Dockers. Mili wore a white shift.

"Ha!" he replied. "Can you believe that Jehovah took that shot at me? I was 'effin blown away at that shite. I never would have expected such immature behavior in front of you, darling. Maybe he knew that Raphael would save my ass, but I'm not so sure. Ha!" The Devil laughed again.

"You seem remarkably well-adjusted considering Jehovah's cheap shot," Mili responded. "I've been pissed off about it all day long."

"So, what are your impressions of the king of the universe?" Lucifer asked as Mili served him a mug of black coffee in a Starbucks' Disneyland mug. Satan stared at the mug for a moment.

"Have you and the kids sneaked there without me?" he asked suspiciously.

"No," Mili answered, pouring cream in her coffee and adding several spoons of sugar. "Back when, I was on loan from the Yard to the Disney folks trying to determine whether or not Walt had had his head cryogenically preserved and hidden somewhere on the Disneyland premises."

"And your conclusion?" Lucifer asked.

Mili put a finger to her lips.

"I cannot say, sweetheart."

"A hint then?" he cajoled.

"Don't be surprised if someday Walt appears down here with a proposal for a Disneyland in Hell."

"Wow," the Devil said awed. "Wouldn't that be something? We have half the population of Orange County here already. That would give them something to do."

Mili chuckled.

"You'd probably have more success creating an ocean and getting those Richie Rich's into sailing."

"Are you kidding me?" Lucifer said acting offended. "We'd have every goddamn Kennedy down here sailing around like Irish royalty."

Mili laughed. It was so wonderful to see that her dear husband was so chipper considering that Jehovah had tried to kill him only this morning. She set her coffee on the table and sat down next to him. She couldn't wait any longer to ask about the slug removed from Gabriel's backbone that she had sent with him to New Babylon for a lab analysis.

"Did you have the slug examined?"

Lucifer looked at her and answered.

"Do popes shit in the woods? Of course, I did," he told her. "But you have to guess what small caliber, barrel-over-barrel, two-shot pistol was used to shoot Gabriel."

"You say that like I should know the answer without having to guess."

"You should," the Devil answered.

Mili puzzled for a long moment. Then answered by naming the only gun like that she knew about.

"A Derringer," she said.

"Bingo."

CHAPTER NINE

oes Jehovah know who Agatha Christie is?" Mili asked Lucifer. It was mid-morning and they had slept late. They were at the kitchen table drinking coffee. The room was homey with plain white cupboards and stainless appliances. The table itself was made of oak and coated in clear Varathane. There were four oak chairs.

Most important was the new Keurig coffee maker on the cupboard. Mili and Lucifer could both live without booze, but neither one could do without coffee. Tea was nice too, but it was a lightweight on the caffeine scale, so they usually only drank it with company, or late at night.

The Devil looked at Mili.

"I have no idea if Jehovah knows who Agatha Christie is. He surely knows *about* her, but only as a resident of Heaven unless he is a mystery fan."

"Which he might actually be," Mili suddenly decided. "He watches *Sherlock* on the telly, remember?"

"Yes, I do remember," Satan answered. "What kind of individual likes crime dramas anyway?" he asked sounding genuinely confused. "I have never been able to figure that out."

"It's the mystery!" Mili declared. "And the adventure! Crime shows have strange characters, violent showdowns, unforeseen consequences, and surprising endings." Mili spread her hands out. "What's not to like?"

"I'll admit that might appeal to some folks," Lucifer allowed. "And all in all, it's certainly safer sitting on the sofa and watching a television investigation than going with *you* in pursuit of the real thing."

Mili sipped her coffee and gazed at her husband. He was smiling, but a subtle tension showed in his posture.

"Has yesterday's incident with Jehovah caught up with you a bit?" she asked.

"I think maybe so. I realized that God was willing to take away everything from me. You. The kids. Our life down here." The Devil shook his head. "I swear that I'm not going up to Heaven again until I have to."

"And neither will I," Mardie said walking into the kitchen in her night robe. She nodded at Mili and Lucifer, then poured herself a cup of coffee and sat down.

"That's not the first time you've mentioned that," Mili replied.

"Seeing God was the single most ghastly experience I've ever had," Mardie explained. "And you'll remember that I once saw a shapeshifter morphed as Barney eviscerate himself on my front steps."

Mili nodded.

Meeting God *had* been a bizarre experience. And she continued to fume on the inside over Jehovah's attempt on Lucifer's life.

"I don't see a way off this case," she said.

"For *you* maybe," Mardie answered. "But I'm not going back to Heaven. Period."

Mili stared at her sister.

"All right," she said finally. "I will miss your presence very much."

"I do feel bad about that," Mardie replied. "Truly I do. But—"

"You are not going back to Heaven. Period," Mili finished for her sister.

"Exactly."

Mili looked at Lucifer.

"How can I get introduced to Agatha Christie?"

* * *

Raphael met Mili when she stepped out of the hole in folded space right in front of God's marble temple.

"Mrs. Morningstar!" the Archangel greeted her. "Thank you for coming. How are you?"

"Frankly, Raphael," she answered, "I am a little unnerved after yesterday's meet-up with the Almighty."

"I am so terribly sorry," Raphael replied.

"My sister Mardie is refusing to return to Heaven, so I am in need of a partner up here."

Raphael nodded.

"Lucifer mentioned your interest in meeting Agatha Christie. I have arranged for you to visit her at her home. She knows all about the famous Wickett sister detectives, and extends a warm welcome to you here in Heaven."

"That is so gracious," Mili said.

"I personally have not made her acquaintance," Raphael told her. "But she is quite a celebrity up here. Jehovah has joked that her books have sold more copies than the number of souls who've made it to Heaven."

"Is that a lot?" Mili asked.

"One billion copies of her mysteries are in print in English. Another billion are in print across a hundred different countries."

"My goodness!" Mili exclaimed.

"Impressed?" Raphael asked. "Wait until you see her house."

It was quite a house. Raphael had provided horses for them and they rode through charming towns and picturesque farms on the way to Agatha Christie's home. Her house was not particularly large, but it was quite imposing. A two-story Victorian mansion, it had large windows and multiple decorative clay chimney pots. The house was made of golden Cotswold stone from northern England.

"It is a lovely house in every way," Mili told Raphael. "But not overly huge."

"No," the Archangel agreed. "But nonetheless, it is by far the most expensive home in Heaven."

"Why would that be?"

"Dame Christie had it brought up from Earth."

"Who could be chartered to do such a labor-intensive move?"

"There are demons in Hell who perform such enterprises," Raphael told her. "They have permission from Jehovah to bring up any commodities that angels or saints desire. For a hefty price, of course."

"I am still astonished that it could be accomplished," Mili admitted.

"Most things can be 'imported' up here. Foods. Garments. Jewelry. Books. Furniture. Electronics. Art. Etcetera, etcetera."

"Is any of it *appropriated?*"

"None of it!" Raphael said insistently. "Everything is paid for *by Jehovah,* using gold that he creates. No one has to work in Heaven. Everyone dresses up and dines. And God foots the bill for it all."

"Including the tear down, transport, and rebuild of an author's stone mansion?" Mili asked.

"In Agatha Christie's case, yes," Raphael answered. "That, however, was a special exception."

Raphael and Mili walked up the sidewalk toward Agatha's house. Mili was sorting through what she'd just heard. Demons were professionally contracted to procure and deliver everyday items consumed in Heaven. How could it be that Lucifer had never mentioned that to her? Mili frowned. Perhaps because her entrepreneurial husband was the owner of the demon companies serving Heaven?

Raphael pressed the doorbell. Mili could hear beautiful chimes ringing inside. A young woman opened the door. She immediately reached her hand out to Mili.

"I'm Agatha," she said in a cheerful soprano voice. She shook Mili's hand quite vigorously. "So, so delighted to meet you!"

Christie was her youthful self of yesteryear. Tall. Slim. Substantial bosoms. Thick eyebrows. Gorgeous wavy brunette hair. She was wearing a long plaid skirt, a white blouse, a gray sweater, and black flats. She made Mili feel juvenile in her green shorts, pink shell, and white sandals. Mili gazed at Agatha's face. She was so pretty and her eyes were so brown. Mili was taken aback. All she'd ever seen were pictures of Lady Mallowan when she was a heavy and white-haired matron in her older years. But *this* was Heaven. Agatha was young again and beautiful forever.

"Thank you so much for agreeing to see me, Mrs. Christie," Mili told her.

"Nonsense!" Agatha exclaimed and grinned. "I am honored to meet you, Queen of Hell's turf. And in more ways than one! Please call me Agatha." She turned to Raphael. "Thank you, dear boy for bringing Mili. I'm afraid you'll have to keep an eye on the horses as there's really no place to have them tethered. A bit of a dilemma. I'm so sorry.

"Please keep them from dumping their travel doo on my lawn and I'll make sure to bring you out a fresh ice tea in short order." Raphael smiled and nodded. "Do you take sugar?" Agatha asked. Raphael shook his head. Agatha led Mili into her house shutting the door behind them.

The house interior was bright with natural light, revealing mahogany wainscoting and solid floral wallpaper, oak furniture stained dark, classic Greek-style sculptures, and large painted landscapes. There were also posters featuring Agatha's book covers, as well as several framed motion picture adverts for books of hers that had been made into movies. All in all, it was a lovely home decorated with great taste. Mili was sorry that Mardie wasn't there to see it.

"Please have a seat anywhere," Agatha said. "I'll bring iced tea for us. Do you take cream or sugar?"

"I do. More than a bit of each, please."

"I'll bring quantities and you may serve yourself as you wish."

Then Agatha was off.

Mili was charmed. She could not remember when a stranger had been so welcoming, so kind and polite. People in Hell weren't rude, but having experienced long, hard personal lives on Earth, most of them were guarded and stern. As things continued to improve down below smiles were more evident. Still, old defenses died hard.

Agatha was not only remarkably chipper, she radiated intelligence. That was to be supposed as she had sold her brilliant books the world over. She had adored mathematics and music as a little girl, and shaped their rigid structures and principles into the literary crafting of seemingly unsolvable mystery novels. Her stories dazzled and mocked the most earnest fans trying to prematurely crack open Christie's endings. She wondered if such rabid devotion brought on nervous twitches in readers, or even blindness. Mili shook her head. Probably not. She sniggered at her little private joke and that was that.

Agatha returned carrying a silver tray with a glass pitcher of iced tea—fresh ice cubes just popped from their trays floated on top—three glasses, silver bowls of sugar and sweeteners, and a large pitcher of cream. Agatha poured a glass for Mili. Then she filled one to take out to Raphael.

"Pick your poisons!" she called to Mili over her shoulder and headed for the door, Raphael's tea glass in hand. Mili added cream and several spoons of sugar to hers. She poured a glass for Agatha and then waited. Agatha returned, grabbed her glass, and dropped into a big overstuffed chair. She gulped at her iced tea and licked her lips. Mili grinned at Agatha's breezy carefree manner.

"Raphael told me that Gabriel was murdered by a bullet from a Derringer," she told Mili. She wrinkled up her forehead. "Imagine that! A big bloke like Gabriel taken down by that wee bit of a gun."

"He was shot through the heart," Mili reminded her.

"And his wound was disguised by a fire bolt that drilled him right to his spine. What do you make of that?"

"Someone disguising their work. Or helping someone else do so."

"And very likely not anticipating that Mili Morningstar herself would discover the ploy."

Mili nodded, complimented.

Agatha went on.

"Guns are not registered up here. Anyone can own anything and until now that was not an issue. However, a Derringer is rare in Heaven. Very few dealers stock them and I suspect no one requests one. I know of a man here who is familiar with most of the gun merchants in Heaven, and he might know who was capable of acquiring such a rare weapon."

"Excellent!" Mili said approvingly.

"On the other hand, running down a killer who not only shot, but also scorched the Archangel's chest, will be almost impossible. Unless—" Agatha held up a finger as if to say listen to this carefully, "—we might be able to wheedle this information from whoever procured the Derringer for his customer. Might be an angel. Might be a saint. Might even be a pair of them working together."

"How soon could we visit the man who knows the gun dealers?"

"As soon as we finish tea, my dear. *And* go to the loo. Though saints have normal bathroom urges, you wouldn't know it if you looked for a public bathroom in Heaven. Further proof that God is undoubtedly a male chauvinist."

"Have you ever met him?" Mili asked keeping her tone neutral.

"Oh, yes!" Agatha answered exuberantly. "Acts so stern, but he's such a kidder. Quite unusual when you compare him to other deities. They're so bloody serious. Judging souls good or evil. Sending disasters of every description down on mankind."

It seemed to Mili that Jehovah was also adept at exactly those behaviors. Yet had he somehow redeemed himself in Agatha's eyes because he could laugh at a joke? Or a prank? Like shooting a lightning bolt at Lucifer? She wondered how Lady Mallowan would react to Jehovah aiming one of those blasts at *her* chest. Which appeared to be ample and firm. On second thought, old Jehovah probably held back the bolts and just enjoyed looking at Agatha's assets.

"Are you willing to walk a couple of miles?" Agatha asked.

"Yes. Though perhaps we could both ride if Raphael will lend you his horse."

"The perfect suggestion!" Agatha agreed. "A horse ride together! On my own I usually just walk to the village nearby. Butcher, baker, chemist, and so forth. Lots of charming cafes and pastry shops. We'll do ourselves a turn in one of those lovely little establishments if we have time later today."

Agatha smiled, picked up the refreshment tray, and carried it to the kitchen. When she returned, she told Mili to relax a moment longer while she fetched Raphael's glass and twisted his arm to lend her his horse. She laughed a sweet high-pitched laugh and toddled off. Mili glanced at a tall bookcase against a far wall. She got up and surveyed the contents. Every shelf was filled with Agatha's books. The spines were colorful and every volume prominently featured a picture of Agatha Christie on the back cover as the book's famous and beloved author. There were twenty or more books on each of the four shelves displaying just the English language editions.

Agatha peeked in the doorway.

"Tally ho!" she cried. "We're off to the village I spoke of. And we're going to interview the chap I mentioned to you. He lives near here and knows everyone who imports any weapon of any description into Heaven. He's eye candy, too, Mili. Which makes a meet-up that much better."

Mili smiled at Agatha's girlish enthusiasm. A gun connoisseur who was also eye candy. She'd be the judge of that. The two ladies mounted and Raphael said he'd meet them back here at the house later on.

The Archangel waved in response to Agatha's wave and called after her, "Who are you off to visit?"

"Charlton Heston!" she called back.

Mili was so startled she almost fell off her horse.

CHAPTER TEN

There were a lot of people riding horses on the dirt path Agatha chose. And a lot of horse droppings. That was inevitable Mili supposed, given the fact Heaven was apparently traversed by horses and not by motor vehicles. She had seen filthier streets in London when she had time-traveled with Mardie to hunt down Jack the Ripper in 1888. There was horseshit everywhere and no one cleaned it up.

Here someone was apparently scooping up after the horses, however. Who got that job? Jehovah with his quirky sense of humor might make the angels do it. Or movie stars. Or reality TV stars.

"Who's responsible for the horse doody?" she asked.

Agatha laughed, quite charmed at the question.

"Kids!" she said. "While it's quite easy for adults to obtain whatever they want in Heaven, children have to do odd jobs to buy things. Cleaning up horse leavings pays quite well. Kids fetch hay and straw for the horses, too, and regularly muck the stables."

"What do they spend the money on?" Mili asked.

"The same things as kids on Earth, I should think," Agatha answered in her breezy manner. "Fashionable clothes, new shoes, music, Starbucks coffee, ice cream, and drugs."

"Drugs?" Mili asked surprised.

"Yes. The usual. Herb. Opium. Some harder ones."

"Children use those here?"

"Yes," Agatha answered. "I am not overly fond of such activities, but this is Heaven you know. Children can get quite bored."

"Do they drink, too?"

Agatha nodded.

"And smoke?"

Agatha nodded again.

"And have sexual relations?"

Agatha chuckled with delight.

"There is no sex in Heaven, my dear."

Mili frowned and thought about that. No wonder the kids were bored. If fate had brought her sister Mardie here at a young age she probably would have figured out how to have become Heaven's first suicide.

"Do you miss it?" Mili dared to ask.

"Well, naturally," Agatha answered. "Though not *everyone* is doing without."

Mardie gazed at Agatha and waited. She didn't have to wait long.

"Do not tell anyone what I am about to reveal to you," Agatha said in a conspiratorial tone. "For a fee, saints and angels can travel through space or time to engage in sex with Earth women or men. Hell's demon network provides such services."

Now why doesn't that surprise me, Mili asked herself?

"Surely such activities cannot please Jehovah?" she asked.

"Probably not," Agatha replied. "But holed up in his temple, he misses a lot of things."

"You mentioned earlier that there are demon enterprises that provide consumer goods and services to the saints."

"Yes," Agatha replied without apparent concern. "Demons are simply fallen angels with hall passes up here, and like I said—"

"God doesn't know about them anyway," Mili finished.

"Precisely," Agatha said.

The two women rode on in silence for fifteen or twenty minutes when Agatha pointed at a small hobby farm down a road to the right. As she led Mili onto it, a mounted figure could be seen riding toward them. Agatha waved and the rider waved back. She pulled her horse up and Mili stopped next to her. Within moments the rider pulled up his horse as well. Mili instantly recognized that it was Charlton Heston, aka Ben-Hur, aka Moses, aka Hollywood's favorite 1960's hunk.

He was tan and his blond hair was thick and unruly. He was wearing jeans, a blue long- sleeved work shirt, and brown cowboy boots. He had a Winchester rifle holstered next to his saddle, and a large pistol of some kind tucked in the front of his leather belt. Heston smiled. His teeth were so white their gleam hurt Mili's eyes. On the other hand, looking at his handsome face made her all the more aware of why Mardie had loved him from the very first time she had seen him in the *Ten Commandments*.

"Hello, Agatha," Heston said. "Heading my way with your beautiful companion?"

"Charlton," Agatha replied. "Mili Morningstar."

Heston smiled again and nodded.

"Your reputation precedes you, Mrs. Morningstar," Heston said admiringly.

"Not much of a reputation when compared to this famous lady," she said and bowed her head toward Agatha.

Heston smiled again.

"Ma'am," he responded, "that would be true if we combined the entire populations of Heaven, Hell, and Earth. So, let's not compare ourselves to her. I will be a matinee idol and you will be Scotland Yard's preeminent inspector." Heston grinned his solar flare smile again, but his humility and humor seemed genuine. Agatha, even though she had been lauded all her life for her genius and her books, blushed in response to Charlton's charming rhetoric.

"Ladies," he went on, "would you join me at the house for coffee and some homemade German chocolate cake I just topped with an inch-thick coconut pecan frosting?"

"Delighted!" Agatha replied.

"Thank you," Mili almost moaned. Dessert with Charlton Heston. Years and years from now, even if she forgot every other detail of this adventure, she would remember that he had served her his own German chocolate cake with inch-thick coconut frosting.

Heston's ranch house was made of redwood logs and was as large as any house Mili had ever been in. The interior had a cathedral ceiling crisscrossed with aged redwood beams, and a huge fieldstone fireplace took up most of a far wall. The floor was covered with oak furniture—sofas, cushioned chairs, tables with Tiffany lamps—and there was a special cabinet with glass doors filled with awards that Heston had won for his acting and for his philanthropic enterprises.

Heston led the ladies to a corner of the great room and placed three overstuffed chairs around a large coffee table.

"Please be comfortable," he said. "Coffee and cake on the way!" Then off he went.

Agatha looked at Mili, a happy glow on her face.

"Have you ever?" she asked.

"No," Mili replied. "And dear God, you don't notice how tall and how well-built he is until he gets off his horse."

"Yes," Agatha agreed and said no more, dizzied by her own secret fantasies about Charlton Heston.

He returned in a few minutes with a tray that held a coffee service for three, a big thermal pot of coffee, small bowls of cream and sugar, napkins, forks, and an entire German chocolate cake. Coffee was poured, Charlton sliced the cake, and he served enormous pieces to his guests. Then he sat and asked what he could do for Agatha and Mili.

"We're here to talk about guns, Charlton," Agatha said straight out.

"No better place," Heston said happily. "And no better topic."

"Are you aware," Mili asked, "that the Archangel Gabriel was murdered yesterday?"

Heston frowned.

"Alas, yes," he answered. "Stable boys told me almost as soon as it happened."

"Have you heard the results of the examination that Dr. Schweitzer performed on the body?" Mili asked.

"I heard that Dr. Schweitzer removed a slug from Gabriel's spine. I have not heard whether it has been identified."

"It has been," Mili told him. "My husband had it checked. Seems that it was shot from a double-barrel Derringer."

Heston scowled with displeasure.

"How humiliating," he said. "I don't care about Jack the Ripper being killed by a Derringer, but a big Archangel like Gabriel deserved to be killed by a *man's* gun."

"Jack the Ripper was killed by women," Mili shot back irritably. "Maybe Gabriel was too."

"Not likely," Heston replied ignoring her ire. "To my knowledge a female has never owned a Derringer up here. In fact, the only Derringers that have ever been acquired in Heaven are the pair that belong to me."

"And neither of them is missing?" Agatha asked.

"I'll have to check," Charlton replied, and without another word he walked off to examine his gun collection for the two Derringers.

"I'm afraid he's a bit of a traditional male," Agatha remarked after Heston had left. "But he is a model gentleman in most respects. He just needs a female in his life. Every man needs a wife to love them and nurture their finer social attributes. My dear Max would be lost without me."

Mili smiled. She knew that Agatha and her husband were deeply in love and that Agatha had faithfully followed her archaeological beau into hinterlands here, there, and everywhere on Earth.

"Why hasn't Jehovah ever been married?" she wondered out loud.

"No one seems to have any idea," Agatha noted. "Would do him an absolute world of good. Polish his manners. Decorate his cavernous home. Create a proper social atmosphere for the many people who seek a visit with him."

Charlton returned carrying his Derringers in one palm. He reached out his hand as though
to say help yourself. Both ladies did. Mili, of course, was familiar with the weapon. It appeared that Agatha was as well.

"So," Charlton said, "both of my pistols are accounted for. The only known Derringers in Heaven." He looked at Mili. "Where does that put you in terms of the murder weapon used on Gabriel?" He appeared to be genuinely interested.

"Empty-handed for now," she replied, looking at the Derringer she held. "May I ask *you* a question?" Charlton nodded. "Gabriel's gunshot wound had been tampered with. His chest had been struck by a fiery bolt of some kind totally obliterating the bullet wound. Is there some kind of weapon that could do that? Or should we be thinking it could only have been caused by an angel's lightning bolt?"

Heston knit his brows and thought about that.

"I've never seen evidence of an angelic bolt used to damage *or* disguise anything. I will say though that at the local range where I practice, several angels practice *accuracy* with their lightning bolts. Smaller than those of Archangels, they are still destructive. Unlike most other angels, these chaps are a bit rough around the edges. Might be exactly the kind of chaps who'd employ their heavenly gifts inappropriately." Heston grimaced. "Terrible thing to consider though. Angels killing Gabriel? Horrifying. This isn't some movie set. It's Heaven, for Christ's sake."

"I think I'd like to visit that range," Agatha said. "Could you perhaps call its management and ask them to contact you when any of those angels are practicing?"

"I can and I will," Heston answered. "Shall we hope that they'll be there tomorrow?"

Agatha looked at Mili.

"Can you visit again? We'll do tea and chat at my house and wait for Charlton's call."

"Of course," Mili replied. "How kind of you, Mr. Heston."

"Happy to be of service," Charlton replied graciously.

"One last question?" Mili asked.

Heston nodded.

"Why would an angel—*any* angel—be motivated to murder Gabriel?"

Heston shook his head, clearly troubled by Mili's question.

"I don't ordinarily repeat remarks uttered behind a person's back, but for years I have heard that Gabriel was involved in a number of on-again, off-again sexual relationships that occasionally sparked jealousy, and even violent threats."

Mili frowned, confused.

"I thought there wasn't any sex in Heaven?" she said slowly.

Heston looked at her and then looked at Agatha.

"That might be the official propaganda, but take it from me, there are couples doing it everywhere up here. Formerly married couples," Charlton smiled and winked at Agatha. "Single couples. Teenagers. Humans. *And* angels."

Mili glanced at Agatha.

"So, the saints don't have to visit Earth for love?" she teased.

Agatha smiled and put a finger to her lips.

"My lips are sealed," she said.

Mili grinned.

"Neither do angels," Agatha mused.

"*Especially* Gabriel," Charlton told her.

Agatha nodded her head. "He was gay," she said.

"That's okay up here?" Mili stuttered.

Heston turned beet red and shook his head.

"Don't mind him," Agatha answered. "Charlton is a dinosaur on the subject. Homosexuality *is* accepted up here. Just not by *everyone*." She nodded toward Heston. "But love is love and that is something that God himself has never forbade."

That surprised Mili. She'd been told endlessly that the Bible explicitly forbade same sex relationships. She'd have to make it a point to actually read that book someday. She looked at the Derringer in her palm. Suddenly she spotted something unnerving. There was carbon residue on the tip of the barrel. She lifted the gun to her nose and sniffed.

She looked at Agatha. She pointed at the gun Christie was holding. "May I?" she asked her.

Agatha extended her palm toward Mili.

Charlton watched silently.

Mili touched the tip of the barrel and then sniffed it carefully. She looked at Agatha, and then locked eyes with Heston.

"Both of these guns have been fired very recently," she said. "Certainly, within the last twenty-four hours."

CHAPTER ELEVEN

Not by me!" Heston said upset. He reached for one of the Derringers and sniffed the barrel. "It's been fired though. No question," he admitted instantly. He opened the hinge on the twin barrels and shook out two bullet casings into his hand. He looked up, troubled. "Both shells are empty."

"Sweet Jesus, Charlton!" Agatha exclaimed.

"I did not shoot this gun," the handsome actor insisted. "I haven't even looked at it for weeks. Not until just now when Mili asked to see it." He examined the other Derringer and cracked it open. He shook out two shells from its chamber. He looked up. "The casings are empty."

Agatha looked troubled.

Mili had no idea what to think.

"Would you let me have Lucifer's ballistics lab examine both pistols?" she asked Charlton. He nodded instantly. "Also, if you could allow me to take a few unused bullets for the

Derringers; they'll be fired and the barrel striations compared to the bullet removed from Gabriel."

"Of course," Heston replied and marched off to gather the fresh bullets.

"He did it!" Agatha whispered. "He killed Gabriel. I'm sure of it!"

Mili wasn't sure how the world's most famous author had reached that verdict so quickly.

"What?" Mili protested. "He's not even gay."

"Not that you or I know," Agatha rebutted. "Big giant sex symbol. Probably did it with Rock Hudson."

Mili couldn't help but grin at that.

Agatha watched her response, and then smiled a bit sheepishly.

"A little too early to judge?" she asked.

"It doesn't mean you're wrong," Mili replied graciously.

"Just a premature ejaculation," Agatha commented.

Mili arched an eyebrow at that.

"Are you sure that's what you mean to say?"

Agatha's expression looked a wee bit naughty, and she didn't answer Mili's question.

Mili laughed, then shushed herself when Charlton returned. He held out his palm towards her. She reached out her own. He poured a half-dozen Derringer bullets onto it. She looked at them. Lead slugs. Brass casings. So small. But Jack the Ripper had had his name written on a few of them back when. And only yesterday Gabriel did as well. She dropped them into her purse along with both Derringers.

"Thank you, Mr. Heston. You have been incredibly kind." Charlton nodded graciously.

"I'll see you again when the target-shooting angels hit the range."

Agatha gave Heston a smooch on the cheek. Mili shook his massive hand.

Once they were on their horses, Mili thanked Agatha, too.

"You've been splendid company today, Agatha."

"It *has* been a delight," Christie responded warmly. "Would you perhaps be able to stay for dinner?"

"Oh my, I'd love to, but I have to check on my three children and ask Lucifer to have his folks examine Heston's Derringers. I am anxious to see what slug patterns show up after bullets have been shot from his guns. Besides, I'll see you tomorrow, I hope."

"Ah, yes. The angels at the shooting range," Agatha remembered. "That will be quite the sight."

"Angels firing off practice lightning bolts," Mili said and shook her head. "Once again,

truth is stranger than fiction."

"Ha, ha!" Agatha Christie laughed out loud. "Even I can't argue that!"

* * *

Pfotenhauer drove Mili back to the kibbutz. She poured herself a glass of wine and searched the internet. She read everything she could find on Agatha Christie. The woman had led an absolutely charming life on Earth, and now she was young and beautiful in Heaven, enjoying forever the rewards of fame, fortune, and happiness.

Pfotenhauer had returned earlier to New Babylon with Mardie. Mili asked him to take the two Derringers she'd brought down from Heaven and drop them off at Lucifer's office.

"Please tell the Devil that his adoring wife insists that he return with you and join his family for dinner."

"Yes, ma'am," Pfot answered respectfully. "Of course, you know the master will do what he wants to do."

"Isn't that the truth?" Mili answered. "Please tell him anyway." Mili reached out and handed Pfotenhauer the two Derringers she'd borrowed from Charlton Heston as well as the fresh bullets. "Give these to my husband and tell him I want both pistols fired repeatedly and the slug striations matched to the pistol from which they were fired. And—while I think of it—ask him to take the Derringers that I own and get their barrel signatures as well. They're probably sitting in one of my dresser drawers."

"Will do, Mrs. Mili," Pfot replied, tucking the petite guns and their ammunition in his suit coat pocket. "Not thinking of shooting anyone in Heaven are you?"

"Bless you, dear boy," Mili responded. "I only ever used them once, when Mardie and I shot Jack the Ripper."

Pfotenhauer knew that story. Everyone in Hell knew that story.

"I will ask Lord Lucifer to find your guns," he promised.

"Pfot?" Mili asked glancing at him. "May I ask where you stay when you're at the kibbutz?"

"I am still devoting my time here to Miss Nancy," the chauffeur answered. "We treasure every moment we have together."

Mili nodded.

"I just found out that both saints *and* angels have sex in Heaven," she told Pfot. "A *lot* of sex."

"Well, I remember my parish priest telling me once after confession that in Heaven there was no marriage. He told me that I should settle down and enjoy a spouse and children on Earth as those would not be available if I ever made it up there."

"But you did not heed his advice?"

"No. I figured that even if there was no marriage in Heaven, my job on Earth prevented it as well. Wasn't about to make any mob widows. I settled into a single life, and limited my relationships to nice women with no expectations of marriage."

Mili shook her head and smiled. She'd heard once that a woman's greatest hope was to inspire love in men. Failing that, maybe a good romp in the hay would be acceptable.

She gazed at Pfotenhauer.

"Did you have feelings for any of your paramours, Pfot?"

"I fell in love with every one of them," he answered. "I swear."

"I like that," Mili replied. "But nonetheless you moved on sooner or later?"

"Ay. That I did," Pfot admitted.

"May I ask why?"

"Never loved any of them *that* much."

Mili nodded her head. She did love Lucifer that much. She couldn't imagine leaving him for anyone or anything. What kept her wasn't duty and it wasn't security. It was because she was still infatuated with her husband and knew she always would be. And that was a good thing, as Hell was guaranteed to last forever.

"Okay, dear boy," Mili said. "Leave word with my Lucifer about dinner and the Derringers."

"Without fail," Pfotenhauer replied, then saluted Mrs. Morningstar.

"Oh! Wait Pfot!" Mili said alarmed. "One more thing." She reached in her shorts' pocket and pulled out a small object. She extended it to Pfot. He stared at it lying on her palm and then took it with his fingers. He looked up at Mili with a puzzled expression.

"Tell my husband that I want a genome map with the requisite number of areas marked, ready for comparison."

"And whose tooth is this?" Pfot asked.

"The Archangel Gabriel."

✳ ✳ ✳

Mili checked her watch. It was already past five in the afternoon. Time to go in search of her three children. Thank goodness that would not be as challenging as finding the individual who had killed Gabriel.

By the dinner hour Mili had Little Mardie, Arie, Sriracha, and Jesus in tow. Off to the kibbutz dining room they went. Mili was ready for conversation. The kids were ready for food.

They went through the buffet line and sat together. Little Mardie and Arie had taken portions of meat and vegetables. Sriracha had taken only meat. Jesus had taken a nice salad with ranch dressing, cooked corn, green beans, and squash.

"No meat?" Mili asked Jesus.

"I'm a vegetarian beginning today," he told her.

"Why?"

"I don't want to think that any animal has to die for my sake."

"What's that?" Mili asked. "a *New* New Testament?" At age seven Jesus had already read the original Old and New Testaments. More than once.

"No," Jesus answered. "I just don't want any animal killed so that I can have a slice of meat."

"All right, son," Mili answered. "Just make sure that you get adequate protein."

Jesus pointed his fork at his rice.

"All the protein I need," he said.

"Not so, Mr. Vegetarian," Mili told him. "You need beans with that rice to make a protein combination."

Jesus got up immediately and headed back to the buffet.

Mili glanced at Sriracha's selection of various meat dishes—beef, turkey, chicken, and lamb.

"Are you making up for Jesus's vegetarian choices?"

"Ha!" Sriracha laughed. "Maybe so, Mom. *Someone* in this family should be tall."

"With all your smoking," Mili replied, "that might not be you."

"Then I'll be the shortest, smokiest, meatiest-eating guy in Hell," Sriracha responded.

Arie smiled with amusement.

Little Mardie did not.

"And who do you think will ever want to kiss you, smokiest, meatiest guy in HellleH?" she said cuttingly.

"Probably the smokiest, meatiest girl in Hell," Sriracha shot back.

Jesus heard that as he returned to the table with a small plate of pinto beans. He rolled his eyes.

"Don't do that around your father," Mili reminded him.

"I would *never*," Jesus protested. "You must be thinking of Little Mardie."

His sister rolled her eyes.

"See?" Jesus said.

"Okay, family," Mili said growing irritable. "I am not enjoying these jabs that you are taking at each other. What's going on?"

Little Mardie, Sriracha, and Jesus all looked down at their plates. It wasn't anything more than sibling banter. A feisty give-and-take. They all knew that. But apparently their mother wanted quieter, much less entertaining exchanges.

"So, I want each one of you to tell me something interesting about your day," Mili said. "And then I'll tell you something interesting about mine. About Heaven. About saints. About angels. And about God."

No one said anything. It was as bad as if their mother had just announced that she was about to hold Sunday school and they were all going. Except for Arie. Shabbat school for him.

"Who's first?" Mili persisted.

"I discovered that there were a multitude of different smokables offered by American Spirit cigarettes," Sriracha spoke up. Little Mardie and Jesus groaned. Mili rolled her eyes.

"Full Body Blue. Balanced Sage. Mellow Yellow. Smooth Mellow Orange. Non-filter Brown. Organic Full-Bodies Maroon. Organic Mellow Gold. Robust Black. And Perique Rich Gray."

"Thank you, son," Mili responded. "Nice to see that your horizons are constantly expanding. Who's next?"

"Arie and I studied Mendel's genetic experiments today," Little Mardie said. "Apparently he fudged some of his results."

"What?" Mili cried, truly offended. Father Mendel had been a great scientific hero to her generation.

"Sad, but true," Little Mardie said. "I can never trust a priest again."

Mili looked at her daughter, only to realize she was kidding.

"Up to you," she replied deadpan. "But if you expect a good car wash down here, you'll have to pay them some respect."

Little Mardie slapped her forehead. Sriracha guffawed. Jesus laughed loudly. And Arie wondered what a priest was.

"Okay, Jesus," Mili said turning to her youngest. "Your most interesting experience today?"

"My moment of enjoyment relates to genetics as well," Jesus answered. "I did a reference check to see whether or not the Gospels explicitly state that Jesus was sprung from God's flesh." Jesus paused for effect. "I couldn't find a single clue."

"That's because he got his DNA from his *human* mother, Mary," Little Mardie said.

"Ah, ah, ah," Jesus responded. "He got his *female* DNA from Mary, but what about the required male DNA?"

"A good question, Jesus," Mili commended him. She didn't mention that that specific question was on Jesus Christ's own mind these days. And that he would soon have his answer. She had Gabriel's tooth, and after Jesus figured out how to get a lock of Jehovah's hair, the last sample required was a snap. A touch of Jesus's saliva.

"What was *your* moment of interest today, Arie?" Mili asked.

"Dinner," he immediately replied. "No one talks or thinks like you guys do."

Everyone looked at Arie and cried in unison, "Aunt Mardie does!"

How Mili wished Mardie could have been in Heaven with her today. Riding horses with Agatha Christie. Taking iced tea with Charlton Heston. Learning about angels who fired their lightning bolts like weapons.

"And now, it's my turn," Mili said. "I was invited to visit Jehovah. The thing that surprised me the most was the way he talked. He spoke like this: **"WELCOME MILICENT AND MARDELL WICKETT."**

Everyone at the table froze. Mili's lowered voice and slurred words had been heard to terrifying effect. Jesus finally commented.

"He sounds truly like the voice that spoke to Job out of the whirl-wind," he said in awe.

"Or the voice speaking to Moses from the burning bush," Arie almost whispered.

"The very voice that sounds through the darkness when it thunders and cracks the sky with its terrible strength," Little Mardie said.

"At least he welcomed you and Aunt Mardie," Sriracha commented. "He knew your names and went out of his way to greet you. I don't think he sounds nearly as scary as Dad makes him seem."

Mili was surprised at Sriracha's spin on God's oddly affected way of speaking. But his points were sound and valid reminders for her not to have a piss poor attitude towards the king of the universe. She shook her head, impressed by what Sriracha had said. From the mouths of smokers.

"Okay, everyone," she said. "Once more."

"TIME FOR CAKE AND ICE CREAM," she said.

"Vanilla!" Jesus cried.

"Chocolate!" Little Mardie shouted.

"Cigarettes!" Sriracha whooped happily.

Everyone stared at Sriracha.

It was just like when Jesus of Nazareth was baptized, Mili thought. Some people thought they heard the voice of God. Most people thought they had only heard thunder. This time Mili's rolling, rumbling voice was heard to offer dessert *or* smokes. Who knew? Maybe that's what God had actually said at the Jordan all those years ago.

She smiled at her wonderful young people.

"Time for cake and ice cream!" she said, and led the way to the dessert bar.

CHAPTER TWELVE

Mili was drinking coffee snuggled up on the sofa and reading Agatha Christie's *Death on the Nile*. She would have been enjoying it more if she wasn't completely clueless as to who had killed the very unlikeable rich girl, Linnet Ridgeway. The suspects she would have pointed at were alibied up to their proper British accents, but, of course, *everyone* on the Nile luxury steamer had reasons to kill the obnoxious young Linnet Ridgeway.

Mili turned the page and her maid had her throat slit. Mili hadn't seen that coming. The young woman expired exsanguinated on the deck of the steamer clutching the torn bit of a thousand-pound note that had been ripped from her hand. Poirot proceeded to identify that rare bill from the wee piece in the dead girl's grip. Bravo Hercule. Or bravo Agatha more to the point. How much fun she would have had in this day and age of DNA tracing and tracking. Endless mystery assassins subject to identification by a careless DNA drop, splat, spit, or spurt.

She put her book down. Oh, come on, Lu, she thought. Call. And he did.

"Sorry, love," he said as soon as she answered. "I wanted at least to have the results for you on the Derringers since I wasn't able to make it for dinner tonight."

"I understand," Mili said appreciatively. "I would rather have had *you* though."

Lucifer's face looked serious on the phone screen. He went on.

"Multiple bullets were fired from Heston's pistols and their barrel markings do not match the slug retrieved from Gabriel's body. The distinct striation patterns on each slug made it very easy to distinguish which bullets were fired from which gun. And again, they were clearly not the same as the marks made on the lethal slug."

"Thank you, darling," Mili replied. "It's odd that Charlton Heston's guns were fired at all. And evidently without his knowledge."

"So he says, anyway," Lucifer replied. "I personally think he's *just* the kind of macho shooter who would never admit to playing with Derringers."

"They hadn't been cleaned after firing," Mili pointed out. "Hardly likely for the gun aficionado who presided over the National Rifle Association."

"Quite right," Lucifer concurred. "Well, then, the identity of the person who filched, fired, and *returned* Heston's pistols shall—for now—remain unknown."

"How did you get on with Gabriel's tooth?" Mili asked.

"I had it delivered to the genetic lab. The DNA was mapped today and thirteen areas were marked for future comparisons. Which, by the way, will be matched against whose DNA?"

"Jesus's own DNA."

Lucifer scowled.

"To what point?"

"I didn't ask, but that seems *obvious* doesn't it?"

"He wants to know who his dad is?" Lucifer guessed.

"He knows who his dad is. He called Jehovah 'Abba' all of his life. That is Aramaic for daddy. What he wants to know now is who his male *progenitor* is."

"And it may not be Daddy?" Satan sassed.

"Oh, be nice," Mili scolded. "Jesus has every right to want to know who gave him life in Mary's womb."

"Be serious," Lucifer reacted. "It's important to find Gabriel's killer. It is useless shite to know who knocked up Mary."

"You can be so rude," Mili said.

"Well, now that you've met Jehovah you know whose DNA makes that inevitable."

"You think you're one hundred percent Jehovah's divine DNA?"

"Yes. Can't you tell by my sarcasm?"

"And your temper, and your enjoyment of bowling?" Mili asked.

"What?" the Devil cried offended.

"Sorry," Mili said. "I couldn't resist."

Lucifer smiled slowly.

"Time for bed," Mili told him. "Raphael has promised to meet me in Heaven tomorrow for another day of searching for Gabriel's murderer. Did you know that Gabriel had a history of somewhat violent ups and downs with his lovers?"

"I did. His most famous squabbles involved Giacomo Casanova."

"Casanova? That despicable old goat?"

"Yes. Most of their love spats took place here in Hell since Casanova is one of the damned. But on more than one occasion Gabriel insisted on smuggling him into Heaven so they could enjoy Paradise's pleasures together."

"I shouldn't be surprised," Mili answered. "It seems that whatever fabric separates Heaven from Earth from Hell is a lot thinner than I had ever imagined. I learned today that both saints *and* angels use demons to bring whatever they want up to Heaven." Mili stared at her husband for a long moment. "Now why does some instinct of mine see your fingerprints all over that?"

Lucifer bowed his head.

"Ever the brilliant detective," he told Mili looking sheepish. "I promise to tell you everything when I come to the kibbutz."

"Tomorrow?"

"I hope."

"Do try," Mili implored. "I miss you."

"Good night, love," Satan said softly.

"Oh, wait!" Mili cried.

Lucifer did.

"Is there any way Jesus can get a lock of Jehovah's hair?"

"All he has to do is ask him," Lucifer responded.

"And admit to him why he wants it?"

"Of course. The Old Man will get a hoot out of it. Now, good night."

Lucifer's face disappeared from Mili's iPhone.

She thought about Lucifer's flippant comment for a long time. The Old Man will get a hoot out of it. This according to the Archangel who'd had that very same Deity shoot a lightning bolt at him. Go figure.

Mili met Raphael where the hole in folded space opened up right in front of God's temple. He was dressed in jeans, a white Polo shirt, and black lizard cowboy boots. She was dressed in white cotton slacks, a gray T-shirt, and boots.

Raphael bowed respectfully and welcomed her back.

"How are you, Mrs. Morningstar?" he asked.

"I'm well, thank you," she answered. "And you?"

"Always the same," he replied. "Though thank you for asking."

Mili gazed at the big handsome Archangel.

"What does that mean exactly?" she decided to ask. She was probably breaking some protocol, but what the Hell? Or what the Heaven?

Raphael answered without hesitation.

"It means I am fit to serve."

"The Almighty?"

"It is the sole reason for my creation. My duty usually has me here, honoring the king of the universe."

"And what did Gabriel do?"

"He was constantly on Earth helping people."

"At God's command?"

"Oh, no, no, no, no, no," Raphael quickly corrected her. "Gabriel had a free hand. God usually steers clear of Earth."

"Too busy?"

"Too disinterested."

Ouch.

"I thought he hears and answers prayers," Mili responded.

"He hears prayers, indeed. And he is very proud of that. For the most part though he lets the inhabitants of Earth—*and* the rest of the universe—reap the rewards of their good deeds, or break under the load of their misdeeds."

"Karma?" Mili asked. "Really? Then how come so many good people suffer and so many bad people prosper?"

"The final judgment of all deeds, if you will, Mrs. Morningstar, remains the joy of sainthood or the suffering of damnation. All in all, pretty powerful arguments for ultimate justice," Raphael replied. "Wouldn't you agree?"

Mili nodded. Though suffering in Hell had largely been eliminated. Unless you counted a person's unhappiness when the Ben and Jerry's shop was out of their favorite ice cream. It was a fact that the truly evil still spent eternity doing manual labor, and the worst of the worst occasionally disappeared into Lucifer's gulag of torture and obliteration.

"Why don't I ever see Archangel Michael when I arrive at these gates?" Mili asked as she and Raphael crossed the giant courtyard in front of the temple.

"Oh, he comes here," Raphael answered. "But not often. My duties are in Heaven. Michael's responsibilities, like Gabriel's, are on the Earth and throughout the universe. As Gabriel had a free hand to bless and reward, Michael has a free hand to punish and destroy. Which he does. A lot. I'm sure Lucifer sees the results of his work show up at the entrance doors of Hell."

Mili walked along thinking about that. Good cop. Bad cop. Good angel. Bad angel. And *Deus absconditus* abscondicating in his god cave watching *Dr. Who* and entrusting trillions of lives to his Archangels' instincts—holy or un—to bless or punish them. Was it equally divine in God's eyes to see good people rewarded and evil doers snuffed? She didn't know. But to her it seemed a lesser calling to be God's bad boy.

"Will Jehovah give Gabriel's duties to you?"

"I don't know. Perhaps. A lot of angels of varying talents worked with Gabriel. Maybe God will simply promote a senior Principality or Ruler to take over his oversight functions. Either of those angels is almost the equivalent of an Archangel in terms of power and speed."

Mili smiled.

"What was Lucifer's role in Heaven?" she asked on impulse.

Raphael arched an eyebrow and looked at her.

"He hasn't told you?" he asked.

"He almost never speaks about his time up here. I don't think he's ashamed, but he's somehow pushed it into a corner of his mind where it doesn't affect him."

Raphael nodded.

"He was God's chief angel." Raphael shook his head. "No, that's not right. He was *Elohim's* chief angel. He went everywhere through the cosmos traveling with the Godhead of female and male divinities who ruled as One. He shone with the brilliance of the sun when he stood next to them, only dimming if Elohim invited someone to behold them. You may recall that Moses once asked to see Jehovah and was told that the brilliance would blind him. That was actually just bullshit. You didn't see any kind of glow when you met Jehovah did you?"

Mili shook her head.

"That's because there isn't any. When Lucifer accompanied Elohim you couldn't even look in their direction. It was like looking at a hundred suns. And it was *only* for the glory of Elohim, the True God."

"So, what happened?" Mili asked. "Lucifer has spoken about Jehovah's binding of the other Elohim and his complete domination of Heaven. He said he could not tolerate Jehovah's usurpation and made the decision to kill him and free the Elohim. Only it didn't work out. He told me that he was betrayed."

Raphael shook his head.

"I suppose from Lucifer's perspective it seemed like betrayal, but the angel who revealed the plot to Jehovah felt that he was only doing his duty."

"Michael?" Mili guessed.

"Yes," Raphael replied. "When Lucifer told the Archangels about his plans to overthrow Jehovah and free the other Elohim, Michael told God and Lucifer was confronted."

"By God?"

"No, by Michael. Once Lucifer's intentions were outed, Jehovah had Michael deal with it."

"And that led to the Great Revolt."

"Yes. Millions of angels lost their lives and Michael banned Lucifer to the distant and unpleasant world you call Hell, inviting anyone unhappy in Heaven to join him there. Fully one-third of all the remaining angels—from every rank—chose to follow Lucifer and abandon Jehovah.

"Of course, Michael controlled the propaganda machine afterwards, so Lucifer was made out to be an evil rebel who was condemned to Hell. And the angels who supported his revolt were banned, cursed, and branded *fallen* angels. Hunted and destroyed on sight by Michael and the angels who chose to remain in Heaven."

"Seems like Jesus hammered a few of those, too," Mili remembered.

"Yes, back in the old days in Judea. But once he figured out the real story he never again judged or condemned the ones who'd left Heaven."

"I have to say," Mili couldn't help but express, "that many of those angels are now demons in every sense of that horrible word. Lying, lazy, ruthless, cheating bastards, most of whom have taken on disgusting shapes and demeanors to fit their immoral and savage characters."

Raphael nodded.

"I've seen their like both in Hell and on Earth. They have assumed the very aspect of their curse. Fallen angels. Fallen into sin. Fallen into deceit, and greed, and every other kind of evil."

"But how can that be?" Mili asked perplexed. "They're angels!"

"Just like humankind, they are made in the image of God. *Were* made in the image of the Elohim, with a range of choices about character, and righteousness, and how to treat others. When Jehovah began to rule with violence and death, we all saw that angels could truly fall." Raphael looked directly at Mili. "You know that to be true, don't you?"

"I do," Mili said sadly. "We had a young woman in Hell ravaged and killed not many years ago. It rattled all of us that a fallen angel had done it."

Raphael nodded solemnly.

"Having had this conversation," Raphael went on, "it should come as no surprise that the angels we will meet on the shooting range are not considered sterling examples of the heavenly beings Sunday school teachers like to describe. These angels talk tough. They look mean. And they act savage. They are utter assholes. What kind of angel goes to the shooting range to polish his lightning bolt skills? Bunch of wankers."

Mili nodded.

"Do you always talk like this?" she asked Raphael. "Sort of gravelly and down-to-Earth?"

He smiled and then blushed.

"I actually practiced to talk like this for spending time with your sister Mardie." The Archangel shrugged embarrassed. "But then she didn't return. Sorry if you feel pelted by the vocab." Raphael's face turned hopeful. "Any chance she'd come back if you tell her that I talk like this?"

Mili shook her head.

"But who knows?" she told the Archangel. "I'll ask."

"I'm chuffed!" Raphael exclaimed. "If that works, I'll be one jammy bastard!"

CHAPTER THIRTEEN

Raphael led Mili out of the temple courtyard and into the verdant countryside that surrounded God's home. Hitched to a tree trunk, three horses stood waiting. Raphael and Mili mounted and rode directly to Agatha Christie's house. Raphael held the reins of the extra horse. It was for Agatha. She answered the door the moment Mili knocked.

"Good day, you wonderful people!" Agatha exclaimed. She stepped out of the house wearing full equestrian gear. A black long-sleeved riding coat, tan slacks, riding boots that rose to her knees, and leather guards that rode up the inside of her thighs to her lady parts. She had on a large white bow tie with long tails, and a black riding cap with a small black bill. She looked bloody dashing was all Mili could think.

Agatha hugged her and shook hands with Raphael. Mili remounted, and Raphael held a stirrup for Agatha while she settled into the saddle. Then the Archangel mounted and the three were ready to ride.

"Off to Charlton's place?" Agatha asked Raphael.

"Actually, he's going to meet us at the range," Raphael answered. "I told him we'd be there by ten this morning."

Agatha nodded and rode out. Mili and Raphael followed.

"I take it she knows where we're going?" Mili asked.

"For sure," the Archangel answered. "She likes to hang out with shooters. Human and angel."

"Doing character studies for her books?"

Raphael chuckled.

"No. She likes to flirt."

"She's married!" Mili responded indignantly.

"Not up here she isn't," Raphael reminded her.

Mili went silent at that. Maybe it was just all in fun for Agatha. Flirting didn't have to lead to sex. Any more than slow dancing did. Which nonetheless her mum had continually warned her about during junior school. Not that it mattered. She'd never been invited to a dance. Mardie, of course, had gone to a lot of school promenades. The only question about her behavior was whether she'd be taking off her scants before or after the dance.

They took a riding trail across a small lovely valley filled with aspen trees south of Agatha's home. Christie outdistanced Raphael and Mili and disappeared from sight. Mili rode on happily at her slower pace, wondering why no one rode horses in Hell. There were many couples riding here. And several individuals riding solo. Most were in equestrian dress. They looked splendid. She wondered if this crowd had their own social spots for drinking, flirting, and talking about horses.

At the end of the valley, as the trail began to ascend into the hills beyond, Raphael pointed at a large two-story commercial building off to the side of the road.

"That's the shooting range," the Archangel told her. There was a huge neon sign on the building's roof that flashed letters in red and white: SHOOT! They rode into a graded dirt lot where some young lads took their horses. Raphael and Mili dismounted. Evidently Agatha was already inside.

They heard loud shooting as they walked toward the entrance. Mili recognized pistols, rifles, and the lethal pop-pop-pop sounds of at least one assault-type semi-automatic gun. Holy Christ. Weapons of war were being fired up in Heaven. No wonder Lucifer was sure that Charlton Heston had never told anyone that he owned a pair of Derringers. Probably equated to having an undersized penis by the standards of this crowd.

Raphael and Mili walked into the building. It looked like a game arcade with colorful neon lighting and a seemingly unlimited horizon of shooting galleries. A whole lot of shooting was going on. It was very loud. Mili supposed that it was music to a gun lover's ears, but the racket made her feel anxious and out of place.

A big-chested, bald-headed man in a yellow short-sleeved shirt with the word SHOOT! printed on the front greeted them.

"Welcome folks," he said in a friendly voice. "What can I do you for?"

Raphael introduced himself.

"I know who you are, sir," the man said respectfully. "But I don't think I've ever seen you shoot here before."

"I am accompanying two ladies," Raphael replied. "This is Mili Morningstar. I think our friend is already in here somewhere."

"The woman wearing a riding outfit?" the clerk asked.

Raphael nodded.

"She said that Charlton Heston told her he'd meet her here to watch angels working on lightning bolt practice. I sent her down to alley seven. Three angels regularly practice there. And they're here today."

The big man leaned forward and lowered his voice.

"I have to warn you that the angels in question work for Michael. They shoot to kill and they keep their skills sharp in this establishment."

"Are they unfit company for ladies?" Raphael asked.

"They are unfit company for any decent person," the man answered.

"Then why are they allowed to use this facility?" the Archangel asked in a trouble voice.

"They work for Michael," the man repeated. "Michael works for Jehovah. Who am I to tell them to take their business elsewhere?"

And you're scared shitless, Mili thought. The din inside the range seemed to suddenly increase. But it was not due to shooting sounds. The clerk saw her confusion and explained.

"You're hearing the bolts being tossed, ma'am," he told her. "Closest sound you may have heard is when a jet plane revs its engines just before taking off. Sort of a loud rush and then a quick release."

Mili nodded. That was exactly what she was hearing. Like air being forced through an airplane's turbine engines at great speed. A sound of awesome power.

"The three bolt shooters are actually holding it down a little bit today," the clerk said.

"They often shoot off their flaming bolts with such speed that we get sonic booms." The big fellow's face turned sour at the thought. "That really hurts the ears."

"Thanks for your help," Raphael said and walked off in search of shooting gallery number seven. Mili followed him feeling her excitement rise. She was going to witness the use of an angelic shaft of fire, the very thing that someone had used to burn a hole in Gabriel's chest trying to obscure the fact that he had been shot with a pistol.

The layout of the shooting range was similar to a bowling alley, alley after active alley, but with six-foot-high concrete walls separating the lanes. Customers were shooting off everything from bows and arrows to bazookas. Bloody damn loud, Mili thought again. Then she noticed that all the shooters wore some kind of headsets covering both ears. They looked exactly like what airplane pilots wore. Fly and talk. Shoot and talk. She went back to the customer service desk and was given three sets of headphones.

Agatha and Raphael were standing back from three angel shooters using alley seven. All of the angels were dressed in Nike workout suits and running shoes. The angels looked like street toughs. Bullies. A white-haired one seemed edgy and hard. A Hispanic-looking angel had a beer belly. The third and last angel had a handsome face with a wise-ass expression. Mili shook her head. Welcome to Heaven. Now watch out.

She stood next to Agatha. Raphael told the two women who the shooters were.

"The tall, spare angel with the white hair is named Allen," he said. "He has the specialized assignment of punishing folks who have swindled people in real estate deals."

"Punishing?" Mili asked.

"Sometimes he seduces the party's husband or wife. Sometimes he manipulates the financing so the deal breaks. Most of the time he forges wills and trusts to arrange for one of his human partners on Earth to inherit the building or land in question. Then he kills the principal and sells the property."

Allen raised his hand and fired a laser-like white beam of light towards a target, a blank, full-size, cut-out figure of a man. The angel's long ray of energy drilled the target through the chest. Right where the heart would have been in a real male. Right where the heart had been in Gabriel.

Agatha leaned over toward Mili.

"He's the one!" Agatha whispered. "I'm sure he did it!"

Mili looked at Raphael.

"Can all angels shoot like that?" she asked.

Raphael shook his head.

"No. There are different styles. Keep watching."

"But how many of them can shoot like Allen just did?"

"Probably ten thousand," the Archangel answered.

Mili turned to Agatha and raised her eyebrows as if to say, he did it, eh? Are you still sure?

Agatha grinned happily. Never hurt to guess!

Anthony, the angel with Hispanic features, centered himself at the head of the lane and raised his arm. He held his hand steady and pointed his index finger at the target. Raphael told the ladies about this second shooter.

"Anthony is an old-fashioned enforcer," he said, watching the stocky angel prepare to fire. "Breaks legs, knees, arms, hands, or takes your life. You name it. If a serious debtor on Earth fails to pay up, he finds himself in a restaurant on fire, or a house on fire, or a car on fire, compliments of Anthony. He proudly says that death by immolation is a proper preparation for a sinner's trip to Hell."

Mili frowned deeply.

"That's terrible," she said. "People are punished for not paying their debts—"

"To Anthony," Raphael answered.

Mili went pale.

Anthony fired a blast of fire, a twenty-foot rush of destruction that resembled the blast of a super-charged flamethrower. Fire enveloped the target and consumed it in a blazing inferno. This angel's firepower was horrifying. He kept his lightning streak fired up until the target had turned to ashes. OMG.

"The last angel is named Robert," Raphael said. "He's the handsome one with the sneer on his face. He has a resentful, disrespectful demeanor and personality. Michael often uses him to beat unfaithful wives, rebellious children, abusive husbands, and loudmouth neighbors. He's a domestic cop if you will. Quick to dispatch a beating whenever he sees fit."

"And how does he do that?" Mili asked.

"Keep watching," Raphael told her.

A range employee set up a new target for Robert. It resembled a wooden man with bolted on extensions for arms and legs, and a round piece of wood for his head. Robert scowled while he studied the primitive mannequin. Then he extended his arm and fired. A single ball of fire hit the target's right leg and blew it off with the sheer force of its velocity. The angel proceeded to systematically blast off the other leg, the arms, and then the head.

"Does that happen in real life?" Agatha asked. "I don't recall reading any stories in the newspapers about those kinds of injuries."

"Very good question," Raphael told her. "Angels with this kind of bolt can modify both the fire intensity and the strength of the blow. Victims subject to such shots on Earth usually look beaten, not burned."

"Beaten?" Mili asked. "As in hurt? Or as in dead?"

"As in dead."

Allen looked over at Raphael and the two women who were with him. He did not like Raphael and he did not want him and his wenches watching him. Had they filed complaints about him? Lost a house or a spouse to his justice? He walked toward the Archangel. Anthony and Robert followed him.

Allen walked right up to Raphael and got in his face.

"What are you doing here?" he demanded. "Snooping?"

"Just observing," Raphael answered calmly and removed his headphones. Mili and Agatha did the same.

"Explain," Allen demanded and pressed his forefinger against the Archangel's chest.

"These two ladies are into mysteries—books mind you—and they read about divine lightning bolts. They had never witnessed them and asked to watch someone practicing with bolts. The service manager up front pointed us toward you and your companions. He said that the three of you are as good as angels get in terms of bolt shooting."

Allen looked a little taken aback by Raphael's compliment. He knew that Michael disapproved of Raphael's role as God's doorkeeper. It's not a job for a *real* Archangel, he often said, neglecting to mention that Raphael's Archangel firepower matched his own bolt for bolt.

"Allow me to introduce Miss Agatha Christie," Raphael continued. "She's a resident and the author of the world's most famous detective stories." He nodded towards Agatha.

Allen stood awkward and embarrassed.

"Do you read books?" Raphael asked, not unkindly.

"I don't read," Allen muttered.

Meaning I don't know how to read, Mili interpreted. Not the smartest bolt thrower in Michael's tool kit she decided.

"The other observer is Mili Wickett, on assignment here at Jehovah's request. She has been asked to investigate the death of our colleague, the Archangel Gabriel." Mili nodded politely.

Allen looked at her carefully. He moved forward and stood directly in front of her. His embarrassment turned to pushy defiance.

"I know who you are," he sneered at Mili. "And it's not Wickett, is it? It's Morningstar. As in Lucifer Morningstar's wife. And you are condemned to Hell."

Raphael spoke up, a fierce tone to his voice.

"You are on very dangerous ground, Allen. This lady is Jehovah's guest and your behavior is rude and unacceptable. Michael will not only hear of it, but if you overstep, he will very likely destroy you. And if he doesn't, I vouchsafe that God himself will."

Allen put his head back and laughed. Hard and loud. He raised his hand and pointed it at Mili's chest.

"On the contrary, Raphael," Allen replied with a sneer. "I will be doing God a personal favor. This woman is Lucifer's bride, reigning in Hell with the disgraced Lightbearer himself. And *you* might want to walk a little more delicately here, old boy. As we all know, you can be killed just as easily by angel's fire as Gabriel was."

Allen raised his hand higher and actually touched Mili's blouse with his index finger. The moment he did a spot appeared on his shirt. Like a red poppy pinned to his chest, a bloodstain spread rapidly out from the center of Allen's T-shirt. He'd been shot. No one could pinpoint where the shot had originated as the range was filled with the sounds of guns being fired. Even as Allen's face registered his sudden acquaintance with oblivion, a second bullet struck Anthony in the face. He dropped without a thought or sound, and Robert took a last bullet shot to the front of his neck and collapsed.

In moments all three angels lay dead on the floor.

Agatha Christie stood shocked, hand over her mouth and trembling. Mili had been initially surprised, but then instantly began scanning the premises for the shooter who'd just killed three of Michael's angels. She couldn't locate who it was. But Raphael knew who'd killed the troublemakers. And then he, Agatha, and Mili saw him together. The calm figure of a tall gunman walked down the lanes to alley seven. He wore a pair of Colt .44 six-shooters holstered around his waist and had just used both of them to administer justice and save his friends. It was Charlton Heston.

CHAPTER FOURTEEN

A re you all okay?" were the first words out of Heston's mouth. He looked at Agatha and Mili with concern.

"Shaken," Agatha answered. "But uninjured. The violent arrogance of the angel facing Mili was stunning. I feared for her life!"

"I'm fine," Mili replied looking up at Charlton. "Thank you for intervening. There is no question that you saved my life, Mr. Heston."

Charlton nodded modestly and looked at Raphael.

"I think that Mrs. Morningstar is very likely correct," he told Charlton. "I have never seen *any* angel act that way. I am baffled as to why he and his colleagues were so aggressive."

"Might Heaven's balance be out of whack with the absence of Gabriel's goodness?" Mili asked.

"It seems to be the only possible answer," Raphael agreed. "What made you react, Charlton?"

The handsome actor answered thoughtfully.

"I knew that you and the ladies would be here as we had agreed to meet up. I brought my revolvers to practice a bit—and to show off a bit truth be told—and I witnessed what came down. Allen was touching Mrs. Morningstar and threatening to kill her. When I saw

Anthony and Robert raise their hands as well, I knew that I had to respond instantly in order to save all of your lives. So, I did."

Raphael could tell that Heston was deeply upset.

"And how are *you*, my friend?" he asked.

Heston's face grew very troubled.

"I never killed anyone in my life, Raphael. I am heartsick."

Raphael nodded sympathetically. Agatha took Charlton's arm and stood close to him.

Mili looked down at the angels lying dead. Blood had soaked their shirts and pooled around their bodies. Who knew how many ages of immortality and power beyond imagination had ended with Heston's three shots? A crowd started to gather as word spread through the shooting range that three angels had been killed.

Charlton said he had never killed anyone before. Mili wondered if there could even be an estimate of how many people *these* enforcers had killed? All by the will and command of Archangel Michael. What kind of creature could he be? So saturated with pain and death that he had condoned the evil deeds of these three angels?

Suddenly Mili realized that both Michael and Jehovah would be furious at what Heston had done. What about his fate? His future? She turned to Raphael.

"What happens now?" she asked.

He looked at her.

"I don't know," the Archangel answered. "I can get this sorted out and the bodies removed, but Charlton's fate is unknown." He gazed at Heston.

Charlton didn't look worried or afraid. He had recovered from the shock of shooting the angels. He had done the right thing by his own code of conduct. He knew that. Did anything else matter?

Raphael sent him home and rode with Agatha and Mili back to Christie's house. Then he entered the temple to have an audience with Jehovah. He had the story ready about what had happened at the shooting range and would present the facts as they were. Would the Almighty overreact and strike him down on the spot? No. Only one Archangel had ever been slain, and Raphael knew for absolute certain that Jehovah was not the one who had done it.

✳ ✳ ✳

"Horrid is far too mild a term to describe the things I experienced in Heaven," Mili told Mardie sitting across the kitchen table at the kibbutz. Her twin had come straight from New Babylon. They were eating cucumber sandwiches and drinking tea while Mili told her everything. It made Mardie feel ill just to hear it.

"I'm sorry I was not with you," she said softly. She had *so* not wanted to go back to Heaven after being shocked and appalled at meeting Jehovah that she had let her sister down.

"I have to admit that I missed your courage and your rowdy sense of humor," Mili responded.

Mardie laughed and nodded. Guilty on both accounts.

"What did Lucifer have to say about all this?" she asked Mili.

"He was really angry that I had been threatened. He knew the three angels who bullied us and called them Heaven's trash. He reassured me that most of the angels in Paradise are really decent and do not have such character flaws. Only the angels who work with Michael. Apparently that Archangel lacks even a hint of goodness. He's been a murderer all of his days, and the angels he recruits become as wicked as he.

"Lucifer was, however, particularly happy about Charlton Heston's intervention and has asked Raphael to insist that he be allowed to witness Jehovah's interviews and investigation of the three homicides. Raphael promised that he'd ask, and however Jehovah responded, Lu said he'd join me if I am called to answer Jehovah's questions."

"Oh, God," Mardie moaned. "You have to go back?"

"I'd have to go back anyway," Mili answered. "I'm on a case, remember?"

"Just resign."

"I never resigned from a case in my life, dear girl," Mili responded.

"Yeah? Well, this may be the worst case in your whole portfolio," was Mardie's take.

"I won't argue that, sis, but I'd still like to see it through."

"You have to tell me why," Mardie replied.

"Because I agreed to take on the investigation. It is terrible that the holiest of the Archangels in Heaven was murdered. I want to know who did it. God wants to know who did it. Put aside your negative impressions about Jehovah for a moment and grant that he authorized Gabriel's benevolent work on Earth, promoting fairness and righteousness across the universe."

Mardie nodded.

"I'll grant that Jehovah has *sponsored* some good things. Still, I would never honor nor obey that warped Deity."

"You don't have to. One of the nice things about being in Hell is that God doesn't care about anyone down here."

"Lucky us. I'm just sorry that you—and by that I mean *we*—have to go back to Heaven."

Mili didn't miss what Mardie said.

"Thank you. I will feel so much better having you near. Plus, you are going to just love Agatha Christie. She's been so keen on helping me look into Gabriel's death."

"I don't know. I think she did it."

"Ha! She says that every time we meet a new suspect."

"Speaking of meeting someone," Mardie responded. "I want to meet Charlton Heston before God lets Michael stick a six-shooter up his ass."

"That's not going to happen."

"Of course, it's not. He's actually going to get his arms and legs torn off."

"*That* might happen."

"Is he gorgeous?"

"Truly. But it was his shooting that won my heart."

Mili's mobile rang. The ID said it was Lucifer. She picked up and his face appeared on her phone screen.

"Hello, love," she answered.

"Hello, Mili," he said. "And if Mardie is nearby, hello to her as well."

"Are you calling about Jehovah's meeting?"

"No. I haven't heard anything at all from Raphael yet. I'm calling because you asked me to have your Derringer's fired as well as Heston's pair and the bullet striations recorded."

"Do you have results?"

"I have to confess that the ballistics folks have apparently misplaced your pistols."

"What?" Mili said in disbelief.

"Charlton Heston's guns are here, but somehow yours are not."

"Stolen out of your very lab?"

"I don't know about that. The ballistics building is large and complex, with shooting ranges, clean room environments, multiple storage units, and a lot of technicians trying to do everything at the same time."

"Don't put a positive spin on this, Lucifer Morningstar," Mili snapped. "Did someone steal my guns?"

The Devil sighed.

"Worst scenario, yes."

"And the best scenario?" Mili asked.

"Well, finding them, of course."

"I am not happy." Mili was bitter.

"And I am not done turning the lab upside down to find them, love," Lucifer promised.

"I'll be waiting," Mili replied.

Lucifer blew her an air kiss and was gone.

"Lu's face turned red," Mardie said.

"No, it didn't."

"Well, it should have. You slapped it hard enough."

"Well, for Christ's sake, Mardie. His fucking lab 'lost' my guns!" Mili said angrily.

"We'll get you some new ones," Mardie offered as a placating gesture. "How hard is that?"

"Not hard, obviously, but what irks me is *why* someone heisted them right out of Lucifer's lab."

Mardie shrugged.

Mili scowled. She called the Devil back.

"Yes," he answered, clearly on edge that his furious spouse had called him back so quickly.

"Was the slug removed from Gabriel identified?" Mili demanded to know. "You didn't say."

"Sorry. I was upset over your missing guns."

"And the answer is?" Mili asked.

"It was a Derringer slug."

"Goddamn," Mili muttered and turned her phone off without saying goodbye to Lucifer.

"Why did that merit cutting Lu off?" Mardie asked.

"It didn't," Mili confessed. "I'm just so angry and he's a convenient scape goat."

"Wow," Mardie said. "That's pretty damn immature."

"Yes. I'll call him later and apologize."

"And you'll just let him stew nervously in the meanwhile?"

Mili smiled a thin smile.

"Maybe," she admitted.

Mardie shook her head.

"Someday I'll have to get married and find how all this for better or for worse stuff works."

Both sisters roared. Mardie got up and took the teacups away. She set two wine glasses on the table and fetched a bottle of Talbot's Chardonnay.

"Wine?" Mili asked. "What time is it?"

"The best of all times," Mardie answered, uncorking and pouring the white wine. "Time not to give a shit."

✳ ✳ ✳

Mili was reading in bed, zooming towards the climax of Agatha Christie's crime novel *Death on the Nile*. Hercule Poirot had assembled the ship's passengers to reveal his absolutely unshakeable conclusion as to who had murdered the beautiful and universally despised Linnet Ridgeway. Mili had no idea who was the killer and that really irked her. Her mobile rang. The ID read Raphael. She answered.

"Hello," she said.

"Hello, Mrs. Morningstar," the Archangel greeted her. "Is this too late to call?"

Mili looked at the bedside clock. Back of two a.m.

"What time is it there?"

"You mean in Heaven?"

"Yes."

"I'm not in Heaven," Raphael replied. "I'm in Hell."

"Why?"

"I came down to strategize with your husband. I have preliminary information about
Charlton Heston's trial."

"Which is?"

"Michael has accused Charlton Heston of the premeditated murder of the three angels he shot at the range. God has agreed to weigh the circumstances that led to their deaths. We have forty-eight hours before

Jehovah convenes a trial—*his* choice of terminology by the way—but I wanted to give you and Lucifer the benefit of a heads up."

"Because?"

"Because you and your husband have been charged as accessories."

"Ridiculous!" Mili said bitterly. "Lucifer wasn't there, and Allen had his finger on my breast ready to pierce my heart with a lightning bolt."

"I *was* there and I know that what you are saying is true. But Michael is offering compelling evidence to the contrary."

Mili scowled.

"In whose opinion?" she demanded.

"In Jehovah's opinion," he answered.

"And that is?"

"Michael claims that on the day you arrived in Heaven you instigated Charlton Heston to kill Allen, Robert, and Anthony while they were practicing at the SHOOT! range. He has eyewitnesses and slugs that were removed from the bodies of the dead angels that he believes are from Derringers that Heston owns."

"Those Derringers were taken from Heston's home without his knowledge, and returned with the chambers fired," Mili said vehemently.

"Jehovah has asked to have the lab results from your striation requests."

"How does he know about those?"

"Who knows? The fact is he does. And Satan is required to surrender Heston's two pistols, which are in his lab."

"Geez, Raphael," Mili said unhappily, "the pistols were in the lab at the time Heston is accused of using them. That can be proved. It's obvious that Heston is being framed."

"I believe so, too," he replied. "And since the actual confrontation that took place with Michael's three goons is the core of the trial, it will be very hard to prove Heston guilty of premeditated murder. He saved all of our lives."

"Did Lucifer tell you that I own a pair of Derringers, too?" Mili asked. "And that they were also at the lab for striation pattern analysis?"

"I know that you own two of those guns," Raphael answered. "I did not know they had been taken to the lab for tests."

"Well, the bad news is that they're missing. Lost. Stolen. No one knows."

"Do you know if the testing on bullet striations had been completed?" Raphael asked.

"I don't know."

"Then let's call and find out," the Archangel said. "Also, please ask Lucifer if the slug removed from Gabriel's body is still accounted for."

Raphael said goodbye and Mili called Satan.

He looked glum on her phone screen. The news was not good.

"Lab personnel told me that both of your Derringers were fired," he told Mili, "and the slug striations were mapped. The documentation, however, cannot be found."

"Paper?"

"Electronic. The lab's computer has been hacked."

Mili shook her head.

"And the whereabouts of the slug that was recovered from Gabriel's cadaver?"

"Missing," Lucifer replied simply.

"Where was it stored?"

"We have a room where transient items—guns, bullets, shells—are stored for return to the owners or saved for a day in court. The slug was removed from that room."

Mili grimaced.

"I will not comment on your dreadful lack of security."

"Oh, thank heavens," Lucifer replied, acid in his tone.

"And I'm not going to comment on the fact that your staff is stealing hardware and data."

"I'm so relieved."

"What I am going to tell you, however, is that I believe that along with Charlton Heston, you and I are being set-up to be blamed for the takedowns of Larry, Moe, and Curly."

Satan looked puzzled.

"Larry, Moe, and Curly?" he asked.

"Michael's three stooges."

"But why?" Lucifer complained, his temper rising.

"Michael's first step is to associate you with the angels' deaths. His next step—and I think it is the very heart of his intentions—is to claim that you killed Gabriel."

Satan stared at his wife. That last part would never work. He knew it but kept his mouth shut. There was no way he could tell Mili what really happened to the dead Archangel.

CHAPTER FIFTEEN

Mili called Mardie and filled her twin in on her theory that
Michael's plotting seemed aimed at ensnaring not only
Heston, her, and Agatha, but Lucifer as well. Mardie was
incredulous that the Archangel Michael was turning out to be a sinister
and dishonest servant of God.

"Why doesn't Michael just try and kill Lucifer straight out?"
Mardie asked.

"He did!" Mili reminded her. "The three toughs in the shooting
alley were clearly instructed to murder me. And when Lucifer would
have tracked them down to avenge me, he would have been shot down
with Michael never having to lift a finger."

"Something still seems cockeyed to me," Mardie said. "The pieces fit,
but not well. And what's with Raphael? He's just standing around with
his thumb up his arse?"

Mili pondered that for a moment. Why wasn't Raphael a target? Even
when he was being pushed around by Michael's angels, he never lifted a finger
to save the women or himself. Mili frowned. Mardie was right. Something
was cockeyed. Maybe Raphael knew that he was not a target. Or *maybe* he
was in the conspiracy with Michael. That was an ugly thought. Yet…

"I want to pick Agatha Christie's brain about the different twists in this case," Mili told Mardie. "They are like snakes, coiling together and darting at me. Swaying like cobras preparing to strike."

"I'll come along," Mardie said promptly.

"Thank you!" Mili exclaimed.

"Plus, we know that Agatha Christie is really the one who did it."

Mili shook her head and laughed.

"Sorry," Mardie answered, her tone unrepentant. "That's just fun to say."

"Can I have Pfot pick you up?" Mili asked.

"Sure. Fifteen minutes?"

"I'll ask him to bring you here and we'll use Lucifer's space step at the house to get to Heaven."

"What are you wearing?" Mardie asked.

"White slacks, red shell."

"Detective casual?"

"Ha!" Mili answered. "You should dress comfortably, too. We'll see Agatha on the sly and be back home as quickly as possible."

"All right, thanks," Mardie said. "See you soon."

✳ ✳ ✳

Mili took another bite of the moist chocolatey cake that Agatha Christie had served with afternoon tea. The Wickett girls were wearing slacks and tops, but Agatha had on a long, daisy-print summer dress with a scoop front and puffy sleeves, complimented by white pumps. All three ladies were sitting in white wicker chairs at a white wicker tea table on Christie's back patio. It was a brick affair with an ivy-covered trellis that shaded them from the sun.

"My goodness, Agatha," Mili exclaimed, taking another bite of her cake. "What in the world is this divine edible?"

"It's called a tiramisu," Agatha replied. "With double the mascarpone cheese and quadruple the cognac."

"Well, it's a sweet contrast to the business at hand," Mili replied. "As I told you, I am now convinced that Michael has hatched a power play to eliminate Lucifer."

Agatha nodded and drank her tea. Milk with two. Mili sipped hers as well. Milk with six.

"The word echoing around Heaven," Agatha replied, "suggests that Michael had Gabriel killed. The lightning bolt scoring was for show, and as odd as it appears, he intended that one way or another it would be discovered that the Archangel had actually been shot. Perhaps he initially set up Charlton Heston to take the fall as the patsy," Agatha went on. "His Derringers were pinched, fired, and returned. I suspect one of those guns was used to shoot Gabriel and that the lead slug will be traced to it. *But then you came to Heaven.* And now it appears that Michael is making every effort to counter any information that you offer.

"Your guns were stolen and the bullet that was removed from Gabriel's body has disappeared. One has to believe that there is a strong likelihood that *another* slug will surely appear and be identified as the one that killed Gabriel, with barrel marks on the slug showing that it was fired from one of your guns. Michael is clearly working to frame Lucifer as a candidate for Gabriel's death."

"What about you, Agatha?" Mili asked.

"Quite right," Agatha replied calmly. "I expect to be named as a co-conspirator along with you in the angel shootings. Not really a death penalty crime I would guess, but I may well be sentenced to spend the rest of my eternity in Hell."

Mardie clapped her hands.

"You'll find that rather marvelous!" she exclaimed. "So much has changed. You have to come and see it for yourself."

Agatha smiled, quite entertained by Mardie's enthusiasm for Hell.

"The biggest puzzle in this whirlwind of Michael's treachery is what does he hope to gain from all of this?" Mili asked.

"That is where Raphael's place in all of this becomes a key consideration," Agatha answered. "If Raphael is unaware of Michael's ambitions, he will sooner or later *also* have to be eliminated. He has power and position, and whatever Michael is up to, Raphael will at some point have to oppose it. Michael is unfit to take over Gabriel's benevolent role on Earth. Maybe he wants to make sure that *no one* fills it. That would mean that the only Archangel working throughout the universe would be wild and violent. Namely him."

"Good grief," Mardie moaned. "I'm getting a headache."

Agatha rubbed her eyes and nodded.

"Me, too," she said. "How wonderful that you two came to chat!"

Mili and Mardie returned to New Babylon none the wiser *and* with their brains fried by Agatha Christie's genius, which was burning at the speed of thought in pursuit of killers and motives.

"So, Archangel Michael is on the front burner," Mardie said, sitting with her bare feet propped up on a kitchen chair at Mili's house. She was on the second glass of the second bottle of South African Chenin Blanc. Two bottles had been sent down from Heaven just today.

"No," Mili disagreed. "Lucifer and I are on the front burners, just waiting to get burned."

Mardie looked at the almost icy white color of her wine. And she read the label.

"This wine has a South African label. Who's exporting it to Heaven?"

"It's who's *importing* it to Heaven," Mili told her. "The more I find out the more I realize that Lucifer's demons likely control all of the commercial shipping in and out of Heaven."

"Oh, my God," Mardie responded. "Are you on the level?"

"Yes. It looks like his demonic host traverses Heaven as frequently and easily as they traverse the folds of space between Earth and Hell. Lucifer admitted to me that he has a virtual monopoly on all products contracted, picked up, and delivered on Earth, in Hell, and up in Heaven."

Mardie wrinkled her forehead.

"Your husband must be rich beyond belief," she said admiringly.

"Well, you could fool me," Mili answered. "He likes our little townhouse, buys used cars, drinks cheap wine, prefers comfort cooking, and dresses in jeans and Polo shirts. Zillionaire cheapskate Warren Buffet at least buys nice suits."

"It's not what Lucifer *spends*," Mardie responded. "It's what he controls. Namely everything that is physically moved between Hell, Earth, and Heaven. That means that no one gets anything *anywhere* unless he and his organization makes it happen. In my book that makes him not only the richest individual in the universe, but also the most powerful. Second only to Jehovah."

Mili stared at Mardie. The reason for Michael's complex plotting and planning against Lucifer suddenly fell into place.

"You've struck the bullseye, sis. Charlton Heston is a red herring. The three dead angels are red herrings. Even Agatha and I are red herrings. Lucifer is the *only* target. He has been Michael's target from the beginning. Michael killed Gabriel and developed an elaborate plot to blame it on the Devil. A devious scheme to get rid of Lucifer *so he could take over his commercial empire!*

"With Satan out of the way, Michael will unite all the angels in Heaven and Hell and run the largest import and export business ever seen in the afterlife." Mili paused, then finished. "Michael covets Lucifer's vast conglomerate, and it's almost in his grasp."

Mardie finished her wine. She stood up.

"Are you getting some more wine?" Mili asked hopefully.

"In a minute. Right now, I'm looking for aspirin. I do not know how you and Agatha can think about this stuff all day long."

"Guts and endurance," Mili suggested.

"No," Mardie answered. "More like jaded brain cells that refuse to deal with anything else anymore."

"Ha!" Mili cried. "That's the most wonderful thing you've ever said about me."

Mardie found the aspirin bottle in the cupboard. She unscrewed the lid and shook out three of the pain relievers into her hand. She drank them down with the last bit of her wine. She looked at Mili.

"Wine now, Milicent Wickett Morningstar?"

Mili nodded happily.

"The one remaining part of my brain that has not been absorbed by sleuthing says yes, please."

Mardie smiled.

The one small part of her own brain that was not exhausted by Mili and Agatha's sleuthing cried out, hear, hear!

CHAPTER SIXTEEN

Y ou haven't been here at the townhouse for two nights," Mili
complained to Lucifer on her mobile. He listened without
speaking. "Mardie sleeps here more than you do."

"I am sorry, love," Lucifer replied. "You know why that is the way
it is without my having to explain the reasons."

"I do know," Mili conceded. "I'm just feeling lonely for you."

Lucifer always tried to make himself available when his brave and
capable wife told him that she needed him. Right now, however, he
was on a 24/7 mission running down information on Michael's plot to
get rid of him. Mili had called him last night and had not only named
Michael as Gabriel's killer, but also accused the Archangel of doing so
specifically to frame Satan for the murder, forcing Jehovah to end his
rule in Hell and strip away all of his cosmic enterprises.

Only today Michael had filed new petitions with Jehovah accusing Satan of Gabriel's homicide. It was accepted by Jehovah along
with Michael's original accusations naming Agatha, Mili, Charlton,
and Lucifer as the murderers of the three dead angels. *Two* preposterous cases. Which might well result in two not-so-preposterous capital
punishments.

"We still have tonight before Jehovah's hearing," Lucifer reminded Mili. "Why don't we have a dinner together tonight and enjoy each other before then?"

"Oh, thank you, darling," Mili said with a sigh of relief. "Can we meet at the townhouse and I'll cook dinner for all of us?"

Satan knew that his wife was afraid that it might be the last time they would all be together.

"Of course," he answered. "Why not invite Mardie and the kids, too?"

"Brilliant," Mili concurred.

"One request though," Lucifer stated. "Absolutely no talk about any of the things we are dealing with."

"Done," Mili promised. "It will just be family time."

"No matter how trying *that* might be," the Devil added.

Mili laughed.

"You experience that, too?" she asked.

"With our wonderful children?" Satan doubled the question back on her.

"None other," Mili answered.

"Yes, it is exhausting having all the kids together," her husband answered honestly. "Bright precocious pains in the ass. But they can't help it. Look who their parents are."

Mili grinned and blew Lucifer an air kiss. He accepted it and smiled back. He noticed that Mili had not denied his comment. What a mom.

✳ ✳ ✳

Someone knocked at the door. Mili opened it. No one ever knocked unless it was a demon delivery from Heaven. Not that that was bad. Marionberry ice cream. South African Chenin Blanc. Mili opened the door. It was Archangel Raphael.

"I am honored and surprised," she told him.

He smiled kindly and bowed his head.

"I am the one who is honored," he said. He was wearing jeans, an Eels concert T-shirt,
and some New Balance athletic shoes.

"Won't you come in?" Mili asked.

"I can't," he answered. "May I have a raincheck?"

"Certainly. Perhaps dinner sometime with Lucifer and me? I don't cook frequently, but I do a wicked beef stroganoff."

"Wow, that would be great!" Raphael said with enthusiasm. "Haven't had that forever."

Mili smiled.

"I have Grigori Rasputin's personal recipe," she said. "The one served to the Romanoffs in Russia."

Raphael was appalled.

"Are you referring to the Czar's psychopathic advisor who was shot, poisoned, knifed,
clubbed, shot, thrown into a river, and then shot again before the friends of the ruling family
were finally able to get rid of him?"

"The same," Mili acknowledged. "Bet that assignment frustrated Michael's assassins."

Raphael smiled.

"It did," Raphael answered. "So much so that Michael had to go and finish it himself. It was good practice for him though. He had to deal with Lenin next. And then Stalin."

"What can I do for you?" Mili asked.

"I am here at the request of Agatha Christie. She did not have another way to contact you from Heaven so she asked if I would bring you a message."

Mili wrinkled her forehead. Those worry lines had deepened in recent days what with Lucifer's life and her own being threatened.

"What is the message?" she asked with trepidation.

"She said to tell you that she has made a major breakthrough in the case. She would like to share it with you in person."

"I can come immediately," Mili replied. "Did she give you any hint of what she has discovered?"

"Unfortunately, no," Raphael said regretfully. "She simply told me that if you were available, to please escort you to the Wickett Sisters Reenactment Club in Heaven."

Mili looked dumbfounded.

"Where?"

"The Wickett Sisters Reenactment Club in Heaven," Raphael repeated. "Pretty self-explanatory I would think, although the club hasn't officially opened yet. That's some weeks off. But rehearsals have already begun for the first play, *The Wickett Sisters in Hell.*"

Mili smiled mischievously.

"I think I might have seen that before."

Raphael grinned.

"It's been sold out for three months," he told Mili. "As I told you when this whole Gabriel thing started, you and Mardie have a lot of fans in Heaven."

"Why does Agatha want to meet there of all places?"

"Gossip mongers are everywhere, and she hopes that seeing you at the club might distract them from the real news—Agatha's break in your case."

"Clever."

"That one word applies to virtually everything she does," Raphael commented with clear admiration.

"One more question and then I'm ready to go," Mili said.

Raphael nodded, trying not to be impatient.

"Who's been cast to play Mardie and me?"

"For the first role, the director—Joseph Losey—decided to recruit two actresses that he knows well and who he thought would be perfect.

Unfortunately, the two ladies hadn't been on speaking terms for a while, so he had to persuade them to share this unique stage opportunity."

Mili nodded. She and Mardie had had a falling out as young girls that resulted in a fifty-year estrangement. If Lucifer hadn't gone looking for the twins' help in solving Hell's first murder, they might never have spoken again. But that was a long time ago now, and they had developed a friendship that was true and sure.

"So, who has been cast?" she asked again.

"Formidable Joan Crawford will be playing you." Mili looked instantly unhappy. "And—"

"And beautiful Bette Davis is cast as Mardie," Mili finished for Raphael. She had gotten the beast and Mardie had gotten the beauty. Son of a bitch!

✳ ✳ ✳

Raphael escorted Mili to the Wickett Sisters Reenactment Club then excused himself. The interior of the club looked exactly the same as the Good News Club in Hell. Spacious with tables facing the stage and a bar occupying an entire wall. There were a couple of actors rehearsing in a mockup of Mardie's kitchen in Hell. Sitting at the bar and watching the rehearsal was Agatha. She waved when she noticed Mili, then hurried over. She was dressed in a long dark summer dress, a lightweight beige sweater, and two-inch heels. Mili had on a plaid skirt, a black blouse, and tan pumps.

"Dear Mili!" Agatha said and gave her a light hug. The kind of embrace that is nice and gentle and doesn't put a wrinkle in your top.

"Hi, Agatha," Mili replied gazing at her. "You always look so proper and elegant."

"As you do as well, my dear," Agatha said. "I'm afraid once British, always British." She grinned. "Thank God we aren't Italian."

"I've always found Italian women to be quite sexy," Mili responded.

"I know," Agatha said. "Bunch of wenches."

Mili arched an eyebrow and looked at Agatha. She was *so* British. Probably wore a chastity belt until she was eighteen.

Agatha swept her arm around the club interior.

"What *do* you think?"

"Deja view," Mili said.

"Ha!" Agatha snorted and laughed. "Precisely!"

"I am actually honored, and Mardie will be, too," Mili told her.

"Please sit," Agatha said. They both took chairs at a nearby table. "I have no idea what time it is down under, but it's the middle of the afternoon here in Heaven. Would you like some biscuits and a wee glass of sherry?"

"That would be delightful," Mili replied. "Thank you."

"How fortunate!" Agatha exclaimed, "since I already sent the bar-keep to fetch them."

She grinned a wicked little grin, as though she had just pulled off the cleverest school girl stunt. She was, Mili thought, just the sweetest thing. With a head full of murder and mayhem.

"Thank you for coming," Agatha said getting down to business. "I have to admit that our director, Mr. Joseph Losey, has modified history a bit here and there in order to add a few extra thrills to the play. Can't help himself I suppose." Christie lowered her voice and leaned slightly towards Mili. "Too many years creating stories with cameras." She winked.

"Anyway, one of his alterations occurs in the scene where Hugh Everett III chases the murderer back into the alternate world from whence he came. In the redacted version, Everett is following as *you* chase the killer in your wheelchair."

"All right. And?"

"And then *you* shoot the murderer with the Derringer you are holding."

140

"Well, I guess that doesn't change too much," Mili said. Though the truth was that Hugh Everett had been the one who nailed the fleeing murderer with several shots from his own gun.

"Indeed," Agatha claimed. "This version is a bit more revolutionary. You know. A lady shooter and all. Smashing good theater for sure."

Agatha went quiet when the bartender walked up. It was Paul Bowles, the famous British author who had lived most of his life in Tangiers. He smiled politely and served a small basket of ginger cookies, two fingers of malt whiskey neat for Agatha, and a large wineglass half full of sweet red sherry for Mili. Bowles bowed and left.

"I got him this job," Agatha told Mili. "He's a bit shy when you first meet him. But lots of ladies adore his craggy face and white hair, believe me."

Both women took a cookie and sipped their drinks. Agatha jumped back into Losey's script changes.

"As I said," she went on, "at the climax, you alone nail the killer with your Derringer."

"Derringers are a bit hard to come by up here," Mili remarked. "I think Charlton has the only pair of them. How did the reenactment folks find one?"

Agatha's eyes went wide and her voice dropped to a whisper.

"That's the whole reason I asked you to come."

Agatha opened her large handbag and reached inside. She plucked out a Derringer with her fingers and laid it on the table. It was silver-plated and boasted an intricately carved pearl handle. Mili instantly recognized the gun, and watched as Agatha reached in her bag again and pulled out a second identical Derringer and set it down next to the first.

"Those are my Derringers," Mili said. "Stolen from Lucifer's ballistic lab."

"Yes," Agatha said. "But they were, in fact, *not stolen*. They were never stolen. Several days ago, Mr. Losey requested that Lucifer loan him one of your Derringers for the duration of the play. Your husband responded that he happened to have both guns in his possession and would clear a loan with you. *And* he'd send them both so as to keep the pair together."

Mili scowled, but listened without interrupting.

"The guns were delivered to Mr. Losey by Lucifer himself a day after Gabriel's murder and they have been here at the club in his possession ever since. After the horrible news of Gabriel's death there was immediate gossip that the Archangel had been shot to death. Joseph had your Derringers locked up in the café's safe where they sat until I removed them just before you arrived."

Mili took a large drink of her sherry.

"How did you find all of this out, Agatha?"

"I employed an angel to follow the gossip and see if anyone claimed to know what kind of gun had killed Gabriel. He reported back that his sources had heard that a small caliber bullet had been recovered from the Archangel's corpse at the hospital morgue. He then investigated what guns might be in Heaven that would be suitable. He told me that Charlton Heston's miniature pistols were the only suitable weapons to have slain the Archangel. I did not tell him that your pair of Derringer's was here at the club."

"Nice work," Mili commented.

"Thank you," Agatha acknowledged. "I have not shared this information with anyone but you. There is, however, one last rather dramatic bit to tell. This angel also found out through his connections in Hell that the electronic data the lab had mapped on your Derringers' barrels *and* the slug recovered from Gabriel's body had been purloined a day or two ago.

"No doubt a slug shot from one of your Derringers would have been presented by Michael as *the* bullet that killed Gabriel and matched to striations caused by being fired from one of your Derringers. But as his minions failed to steal the guns themselves, you've lucked out."

"Yes," Mili said. "If Michael cannot access my guns, thus failing to connect them to the bullet that killed Gabriel, then it is impossible for him to claim that the Devil used them."

Mili was thrilled that Agatha and her angel spy had completed such sterling work on her missing Derringers and was pleased that Lucifer might avoid Michael's effort to take him down. Now maybe she could get back to the crisis that had brought her to Heaven in the first place. Who killed the Archangel Gabriel?

CHAPTER SEVENTEEN

After Agatha shared her revelations, she and I went to visit Charlton Heston and told him about Agatha's discovery of *my* Derringers up in Heaven," Mili told Mardie. They were seated in Mardie's kitchen. Drinking. Mili was having some white wine and Mardie had fixed herself a Crown Royal Perfect Manhattan. What are you up to, Hugh Everett, she wondered.

Mili had arrived back from Heaven in the late afternoon and had sent Pfotenhauer to the kibbutz to fetch Little Mardie, Sriracha, and Jesus for a family dinner tonight. She and Lucifer had talked on the phone again, but she had not mentioned that Agatha had tracked down her "stolen" Derringers in Heaven. The conversation had been somewhat frosty, but Lucifer didn't ask what was bothering his wife.

Mardie poured more wine for Mili and fixed herself another Manhattan. She sat down again and asked Mili a question.

"If you and Agatha are correct in assuming that Michael's attempt to frame Lucifer with Gabriel's murder has indeed had the bottom fall out of it, why doesn't he simply drop the request for Jehovah to judge Lucifer's guilt? Unless Michael has an eyewitness to the shooting there is absolutely nothing that he can use to connect Lucifer to the Archangel's murder."

"I can't believe I have to go back there tomorrow for the hearing," she said.

"You have no choice," Mili reminded her.

"Boy, do I know that," Mardie answered. "Doesn't mean I'm looking forward to it."

"Right now, it's shaping up to be a pointless exercise in Archangel shenanigans. Gabriel's death has had some kind of liberating effect on Michael, but his dual charges against Lucifer and us won't hold water. My guess is that Jehovah will throw them out and turn on the telly."

Mardie shook her head with disgust.

"I am sorry to say this," she said, "but I think I liked the way I *used* to think about God."

Mili arched an eyebrow.

"What? You didn't used to think about God," she reminded her.

"Not as an adult," Mardie said. "Ignorant bliss for sure. But I did think of him when I was a little kid. Had him on a throne in Heaven with white hair and a bushy beard. Was sure that he didn't know my name. But who cares, I thought, whenever anyone ever mentioned him." Mardie's face took on a fearful expression. "But now it's different. I've seen Heaven. I'm afraid. God is irrational and arbitrary. Aloof from reality in every way. The thought of *that* Deity running the universe fills me with anxiety and dread."

"I don't know what to say, sis," Mili replied. "Working on Gabriel's case is the most nerve-wracking investigation I've ever experienced. Yet no matter the circumstances, I am determined to honor the Archangel's memory by finding out who killed him. We have some of the important pieces sorted. Namely that he was killed by a small caliber bullet, the wound was disguised after he died, and that he left behind some unhappy lovers."

"All you're missing is the who and the why," Mardie said sarcastically. "Was it Casanova? Infuriated by being dumped? Or was it

James Dean? Young and good-looking and pissed off at being ignored? Perhaps it was Michael himself, determined after all of these ages to get rid of the other Archangels, and maybe even take on Jehovah himself? Net result of *that* loss might only be one less television viewer during the Nielsen sweeps."

Mili shook her head. She was not giving up and she wasn't the only one.

"Agatha Christie is turning Heaven upside down," she claimed. "Asking questions and following leads. She is confident, thorough, and brings a brilliant, unclouded mind to the pursuit of answers."

Mardie looked at Mili.

"Should I open another bottle of wine?" she asked.

"If you would be so kind," Mili replied. "Thank you. Do you have any biscuits?"

"Cookies?" Mardie asked. "With wine?" She stuck out her tongue.

"I was thinking of cookies with cookies," Mili answered.

"Too much sugar and you'll be diluting *your* cloudless mind," Mardie warned.

"Not any more than you and your endless Crown Royal Perfect Manhattans," Mili shot back.

"Clueless, not cloudless," Mardie proposed. " *That's* me."

"We're *both* clueless," Mardie agreed. "The Wickett sisters in trouble."

"Oh!" Mardie cried. "I almost forgot." She rose and returned with a sealed postal envelope and handed it to Mili. "Speaking of clueless, Jesus brought this by for you yesterday. You were at the kibbutz and I just forgot about it."

"What is it?" Mili asked. "Do you know?"

"Nope. He simply asked me to give it to you first chance."

Mili lifted the envelope flap and removed a small plastic baggie. She held it up and inspected the contents. Two cotton swabs. Of course, she remembered. Jesus had asked for DNA comparisons between his genome and Gabriel's, *and* between his and Jehovah's. She'd forgotten. Jesus had not. He'd probably been thinking about this for a couple of thousand years.

She'd had Pfotenhauer deliver Gabriel's tooth to Lucifer for DNA tests and he had told her that they had been done. No reason the Devil couldn't take Jesus's swab samples by the genetics lab on his way to his office after dinner. That meant all she needed was a lock of Jehovah's hair to complete the testing. Piece of cake. Right.

* * *

There was absolutely no consensus among Mili's kids as to what she should prepare for dinner. Each child insisted on their favorite dish, expressing great revulsion at the thought of having to eat someone else's favorite. Even Lucifer said that he felt entitled to ask for steak and fries since it could well be his last meal. Mili refused to dignify that comment with a response. She also finally just refused to cook. She asked the Devil if they could take the family out for dinner at Oscar's Smorgasbord, a favorite New Babylon restaurant that everyone loved.

Mili knew that there really was an Oscar. Oscar Klemet Ivar Preus. He was a Norwegian immigrant who'd grown up on his father's farm in Pipestone, Minnesota. He'd lost four fingers when they froze one winter day while he was dairy milking in the middle of a record-breaking cold spell of negative fifty-seven degrees. His fingers just snapped away, dropping onto a pile of frozen cow teats that had broken off as well. It took Oscar a while to figure which ones were his fingers until he landed on the device of picking out the ones that had fingernails.

Oscar left home at sixteen and signed with a crew operating a Seattle crabbing boat in the Alaskan Bering Sea. The boat was owned and captained by his uncle Jacob. Oscar ordered the food supplies and did the cooking. It was hard work in stormy seas, but the pay was lucrative and he performed his tasks without complaint. Then one bitterly cold January the Bering Sea became subject to high waves and temperatures as extreme as those he had experienced in Pipestone. The ship was swamped and the crew abandoned it. After twenty hours on a lifeboat they were rescued, but three more of Oscar's fingers had turned to ice and were lost when his frozen gloves were yanked off.

Down to three working fingers, Oscar discovered that he could still cook and decided to open a small cafe in Seattle. He ran it successfully for many decades without losing any more digits. His Smorgasbord specialties attracted Nordic diners from all over the Pacific Northwest, and his café grew into a huge establishment overlooking Lake Union. He retired rich and died happy. In Hell, he opened another Oscar's Smorgasbord and reaped fame and wealth all over again.

Jesus asked his mother what a smorgasbord was. It's like the kibbutz buffet, Mili told him. Ymm, he said. Pfot drove her and the children to Oscar's and Lucifer followed them on his Harley Wide Glide. His last dinner and his last ride, he thought morosely. After dinner, maybe he'd even follow Sriracha outside and bum his last smoke.

The Morningstar family ate together at a grand table. Mili looked at everyone's selection. Little Mardie had picked a shrimp salad and a side of Caprese, which was mozzarella cheese with beefsteak tomato slices. Sriracha had placed three breaded and deep-fried corndogs on his tray. Mili wasn't surprised. Oscar himself had once noticed Sriracha's selection and told him that *he* had had his first corndog at the Minnesota State Fair and to this day when he ate at the restaurant, he never looked farther down the buffet offerings than the corndogs.

Jesus had taken thick slices of lamb, beef, and turkey. Mili had to ask why he was eating meat again. He said he wasn't eating meat, sounding offended. All of these foods had been raised eating grasses or corn or grains. He regarded them as vegetables in a final form. Evolved. Like Pokémon.

Lucifer had a thick New York strip steak cooked rare and a pile of Julienne-cut French fries. He ate with determination, savoring every bite as though he were indeed eating his last meal. Mili felt sorry for him. She knew that he was stressed over having to see Jehovah tomorrow. But she didn't say anything to him. She was still steamed that he had lied to her and had taken her Derringers without permission.

Speaking of steamed, she had filled her own plate with steamed clams, oysters, muscles, and abalone, the likes of which were never offered at the kibbutz's kosher cafeteria. She also had a small bowl of melted butter, a rich and welcome addition to her seafood that was never served with meat at the kibbutz either. She was sharing a bottle of Napa Valley Silver Oak Cabernet Sauvignon with Lucifer. Maybe not perfect for seafood, but this was Hell. You did whatever you wanted. And she never wanted to be anywhere else.

"Okay, you wonderful people," she said to her family. "What shall we talk about?"

Jesus spoke up immediately.

"My Hebrew school teacher told me that you and Father have been summoned to appear before Jehovah concerning the deaths of several angels in Heaven."

Mili sat absolutely stunned.

Lucifer replied immediately.

"Did any of the rest of you hear things like that today?" he asked the children.

Little Mardie nodded. So did Sriracha.

"Well, here's the scoop," their father told them. "You know that your mother and Aunt Mardie were invited by Jehovah himself to investigate the murder of Archangel Gabriel. Quite a vote of confidence from God, wouldn't you say? Another Archangel has complained about both your mother and me to Jehovah, but his concerns are made up and he knows that. Yes, God wants some answers—which he will get—and everything will be fine."

Little Mardie was visibly relieved. Mili was so grateful to her husband that she instantly forgave his double-dealings with her. Not that he wouldn't still hear about them later.

"I hope you're right, Father," Jesus spoke up. "Everything I've read about Jehovah seems to indicate that he is quick to judge and slow to forgive."

"How does that make you feel about him?" Mili asked.

"I've never known anyone like that down here," Jesus replied, obviously a little shaken that his dad had been summoned to testify before such a deity. "I can only pray that in his wisdom God will listen and exonerate the innocent."

"Well said, son," Lucifer told him. "In all the time I have known Jehovah, I have never seen him punish an innocent person. It is perhaps his most commendable trait."

"Then why are you in Hell?" Jesus asked.

"Because I was not innocent," Lucifer answered bluntly.

"What did you do?" Sriracha asked, finding this turn in the table conversation disturbing and fascinating.

"It is not a tale for tonight," Lucifer said firmly. "But I promise you—with your mother as my witness—the day will come when I will share the story of what happened that put a permanent wedge between Jehovah and me. One thing I *will* tell you now. The rift was all my doing."

It grew very quiet at the table, and everyone ate in silence for a few minutes. Satan was hugely admired by his wife and children, and his honest admission of wrongdoing was devastating. All three children had been subject to whispered bits of gossip at the kibbutz about the Lord of Hell's attempt to dethrone Jehovah. To have heard its confirmation from Lucifer's very lips, however, was an emotional tsunami that swept his children into a state of fear and amazement.

Clearly Lucifer had survived an ancient rebellion, and God had assigned the management of Hell to him as an apostate Archangel. But

Little Mardie, Sriracha, and Jesus were all fearful that he was once again required to appear before God to answer *new* charges. How they longed to believe their father's reassuring statements that all would be well.

Dinner slowly got back to normal. Whatever might happen tomorrow was relegated to a deep unease in Mili's heart, and a longing for all of it to be over. There was dessert and coffee. Lucifer and Sriracha disappeared for a while and they both came back smelling like smoke.

Oscar himself dropped by their table to say hello. He was a tall, older, white-haired man with a craggy weathered face like the old Norse winter Christmas figure Sinterklaas. Santa Claus to everyone else. He shook hands with Lucifer and greeted Mili and the children by name. They frequently dined together at his smorgasbord. Oscar asked the Devil's permission to perform a little magic show he'd been working on. Lucifer twirled his hand in a grandiose way and said, "Proceed!"

Oscar did card tricks and ventriloquism with cups and saucers talking back and forth, then with a slight-of-hand he made those same cups and saucers disappear. His routines were sweet and his simple feats amusing. Oscar had saved his biggest trick of all to surprise Lucifer and his family.

He rolled up a tall box on wheels that looked like a coat cabinet with a curtained opening. He said some magic words, waved his right hand with its two remaining fingers, then pulled open the curtain. Out stepped Lucifer, Mili, and all three Morningstar children! Shapeshifters!! Everyone gasped, and then cried out with surprise and delight.

The five demons shed their disguises and appeared in their natural red skins. The restaurant's patrons jumped to their feet, clapped, and cheered wildly. The shapeshifters bowed proudly again and again. Even Oscar took a well-deserved bow.

Back at home everyone stayed up late. It had been a wonderful night and no one wanted it to end. Plus, little fears had begun to dance again in the back of their minds about what tomorrow might bring.

Would its consequences change their lives forever? It might have been a good thing if everyone had told each other how happy they were with each other. And how much they truly loved each other. But they did not. It was not that they didn't want to. But the very idea of saying I love you out loud seemed like the very thing that would jinx them all. Exposing their family and destroying the happiness they wanted so desperately to hold on to forever.

Mili and Lucifer went to bed before the kids. Not that they were willing to risk speaking the forbidden words of longing and love either. But that didn't stop them from being close. Actions, as they say, are stronger than words.

Mili went to sleep depressed. She had not solved the mystery of Gabriel's murder and it felt like an empty hole in her heart. She had nowhere else to go. Nothing new to explore. She felt defeated. Her hopes about partnering with Agatha Christie any further seemed futile, and she was hoping with all of her heart that she and Lucifer were not doomed as well. She felt dread about tomorrow down to her toes. All ten of them.

CHAPTER EIGHTEEN

 J ehovah stood in front of his recliner and the giant screen television was off. The Archangel Raphael stood at his side. Six other
individuals were standing in a semicircle facing him. Lucifer. Mili.
Mardie. Agatha Christie. And Charlton Heston. Archangel Michael
was also present, but stood apart from the others, but was facing God
all the same.

Lucifer wore a metallic-silver robe with gold trim on the neck,
hem, and cuffs. Mili and Mardie had on formal black dresses, covered
shoulders, and black flats. Agatha had on a black and brown striped
dress to her ankles and a black sweater. Charlton Heston had on a
navy-blue suit, white shirt, and burgundy tie.

Michael wore a gold robe with hundreds of rubies and sapphires
emblazoned on the chest. The Archangel was extraordinarily tall. Mili
judged that he must be almost eight feet tall. His black hair was cut
in a short crew, and he had a sallow, unhealthy complexion. He had
coal-black eyes and heavy eyebrows.

It looked like his face was set in a permanent scowl, but it might
have just been the way the deep lines in his cheeks made him appear.
Mili remembered that he had on occasion visited with Lucifer in

Hell, but she had never exchanged words with him. There were a few choice comments that she wouldn't mind sharing with him right now.

Jehovah was wearing a white cotton sweat suit. Ready to take on whichever Archangel survived today's audience? Boxing? Running? Arm-wrestling? His long black hair fell down his shoulders in thick waves. That was different than before, Mardie thought. Well, god-damn. She realized that the king of the universe used a curling iron. And he looked like Greg Hemphill, the handsome star of Scottish BBC's *Still Game*. Not hard to guess what the Almighty had been watching on the telly before everyone arrived.

The Lord had a pleasant expression on his face, as though this was just an impromptu gathering of old friends. Maybe that's how it felt to him. Mardie was sure it was more like a mob of killers. The only person in this group who had not shot down someone in cold blood was Agatha Christie.

God began the hearing.

"Thank you for being prompt." He spoke in an ordinary male baritone voice. Mili felt instant relief. No games. No thunderous voice. Just God getting to the bottom of things. "Let us begin." He looked at Michael. "You have asked for this meeting. Start by stating why we are here."

Michael answered in a confident tenor voice.

"I actually have to request a postponement, Great Jehovah. I orig-inally pressed charges believing that Gabriel had been shot by Lucifer using his wife's Derringer. But the gun has disappeared, along with a record of the striations of the barrel nicks etched onto its fired bullets. Missing as well is the slug recovered from Gabriel's corpse."

"Then you have no case," God said.

"I have no *evidence*," Michael answered. "The accused has success-fully disposed of it."

Mili scowled, but remained silent.

Jehovah gazed at Michael, but did not challenge his charge citing Lucifer's involvement in concealing evidence.

Agatha Christie raised her hand.

"May I speak?" she politely asked Jehovah.

"Of course," God answered and smiled cordially. He had never read any of Christi's works, but he admired the fact that her books had sold almost as many copies worldwide as the Bible. God-given talent he called that.

"It has been my pleasure to have worked with Mili Morningstar and Mardie Wickett," Agatha began, "as they investigated the tragic death of the Archangel Gabriel." Christie's face was kind and her voice was pleasant and easy to listen to. "May I point out first, Lord, that not only did Lucifer *not* dispose of his wife's miniature pistols, he delivered them here to Heaven at the request of Joseph Losey, the director-in-residence at the Wickett Sisters Reenactment Club."

"Have I met him?" Jehovah asked and wrinkled his brow.

"I don't know, Lord, but you are more than welcome to attend any reenactment and I'll introduce you to him. An American ex-pat who directed brilliant European films."

Jehovah nodded benignly.

TMI, Mardie thought. The Almighty had never seen a European film in his life.

"Mrs. Morningstar's matching Derringers were both in Mr. Losey's safekeeping."

Michael's ugly scowl appeared to have deepened, but he remained silent.

Agatha stepped slightly forward.

"From the very beginning of this case I have been struck by the unexplained nature of Gabriel's death."

Agatha looked directly at Jehovah.

"If I may start from the very beginning?"

Jehovah nodded. He was interested in what Agatha had to say.

"Gabriel's body was discovered, apparently shot in the chest by a lightning bolt. He was found lying in the courtyard of your temple, Lord. How odd was that, I questioned, when Mili told me about that discovery. How could the great and mighty Archangel be murdered on the very grounds of God's house? Apparently struck down by an angel's lightning bolt?"

Agatha turned her gaze to Raphael.

"Archangel Raphael was led to the dead body. Not a surprise since he stands nearby, guarding our Heavenly Father night and day. Yet, where was he when Gabriel was slain? He was close enough to have seen it. Did he, in fact, actually witness the assassination? Yet he has never said a single word about the death of his friend. Why not?"

Raphael did not speak. His face was emotionless.

Agatha went on.

"It was thanks to Mili's insistence that Gabriel's body was carefully examined. It turned out that fire bolt shot to the Archangel's chest was a ruse. He had been shot by a *pistol* first, and the bullet that killed him was found lodged in his spine by Dr. Albert Schweitzer in the hospital morgue. As enlightening as this find was, Mili was not able to narrow down the murderer to a member of the saints in Heaven, nor whichever angel—or Archangel—had administered the lightning bolt that blasted open Gabriel's chest, done to obscure the fact that there was a bullet in his backbone. A bullet shot by a Derringer. But whose Derringer?"

Agatha paused, and then continued, her voice ever so slightly more intense.

"I found it strange and somewhat cavalier that Lucifer lent his wife's Derringers to Mr. Losey without consulting her. Further, the tests that she requested on the guns—ballistics tests to see if they matched the barrel marks on the slug recovered from Gabriel's cadaver—were performed *only* to have the results hacked and removed from Hell's lab computer. What?"

Agatha spread her arms wide and wore an astonished look on her face.

"Stolen? And not only the test results, but the very slug that had killed Gabriel *went missing as well.*"

Agatha shook her head, frowning. Then she spun and extended her arm, pointing her hand at Lucifer.

"Lucifer Morningstar what were you thinking?" she asked in a shrill voice. "Based on these circumstances alone a good case could be made for your deliberate participation in covering up the truth of Gabriel's murder." Agatha paused. Mardie felt faint. Mili was furious. "Were you protecting someone?" Agatha asked in a loud voice. "Or were you just protecting yourself?"

Satan flushed deep red, but kept his lips sealed.

Agatha watched him carefully. Then she turned and faced Archangel Michael.

"During the whole time Mili and Mardie investigated means and motives of Gabriel's killer, you showed no interest, Michael. You never offered support. You never even welcomed them though they were here at the express invitation of Almighty God himself. Did you really care so little for Gabriel? Or have such a small interest in his murderer? Evidently. You never showed any upset over your colleague's foul murder.

"Nor did you demand an explanation from Raphael about what he might have witnessed. And you didn't bother to talk to Lucifer even when you discovered that he had *misplaced* the likely murder weapon, the map of its barrel marks, and the very slug that killed Gabriel. Very pacifistic for the Archangel of God's righteousness and the instrument of his justice across the universe!"

Agatha looked Michael in the eye.

"Wouldn't you say?" she asked sharply.

"Preposterous!" snapped Michael. "What possible reason could I have for not caring about who killed Gabriel?"

Agatha responded in an emotionless voice.

"I didn't say that *you did not care*. I said you did not show any emotion, nor pursue any road that might lead to his killer. But that is completely understandable, isn't it? *Because maybe you already held the answers to Gabriel's death.*"

Michael raised his hand and aimed at Agatha.

Jehovah himself cried out.

"STAY THY HAND SERVANT!"

Michael dropped his arm and hung his head.

"I deny her accusation, Jehovah!" he said vehemently.

Jehovah watched him for a long moment. Then he looked at Agatha Christie.

"You're not done yet, are you?" he asked.

"No, Lord God. But I am close."

Jehovah nodded and Agatha continued.

"So, Raphael has been silent. Lucifer has gotten rid of the murder weapon, the tests that would confirm such, *and* the bullet it shot into Gabriel. And lastly, Michael failed to say anything at all about the murder, neither offering support nor vengeance.

"Everything I have presented is based on circumstantial deductions, but they have been made possible by the facts unearthed by the detective work of the Wickett sisters, and the actions—or the lack of actions—by the Archangels *demand that we acknowledge the glaring and absolute complicity of the three Archangels to cover-up the circumstances of the murder of their unfortunate brother and colleague, the Archangel Gabriel.*"

Agatha paused a long moment. Then she looked directed at Jehovah and continued.

"These three Archangels know who murdered Gabriel. Because they are the ones who killed him."

Gasps of disbelief filled the room. Even God looked astonished at Agatha Christie's charge. She quickly explained.

"My conclusions make it inescapable to acknowledge that somehow the Archangels shot Gabriel, moved his body, and disguised his wound. Alas, I cannot prove it." She glanced at the three Archangels in turn. "Therefore, I implore you three in the name of the Living God to throw yourselves on his abundant mercy and confess what happened."

No Archangel spoke.

Then God spoke.

"GUILTY OR INNOCENT WHO WILL SPEAK?"

Michael looked at Jehovah and stepped forward.

"I shot Gabriel," he said. The group was stunned. Everyone except for Agatha. "I swear

by your throne, king of the universe, that it was an accident. Both Raphael and Lucifer can attest to it. Both were eyewitnesses to the horrible tragedy."

Raphael and Lucifer nodded solemnly.

Michael continued.

"On occasion, all four of us Archangels gathered to play cards. Three nights ago, we were in a lounge in a faraway galaxy gambling. We were happy to be together and we drank heavily. Lucifer grinned and pulled a Derringer out of his pants pocket. He waved it around. We knew what it was, but not why he'd brought it.

"'What are you doing with that toy?' I asked."

"'Showing off the weapon my little woman used to kill Jack the Ripper,' Satan said."

Mili glared at Lucifer. *Little woman?* Satan refused to look back at her.

"Gabriel laughed out loud," Michael continued. "'What?' he cried. 'She killed fearsome Jack the Ripper with that little stinger?'

"I laughed, too, and grabbed the gun away from Lucifer. I pointed it right at Gabriel's

chest and said, 'Want to see what this little stinger can do?' Raphael tried to knock the gun out of my hand and it went off. I shot Gabriel. He looked surprised, then he fell from his chair. Dead.

We all were shocked and, to be honest, panicked at what you would do to us, Lord. We moved Gabriel's body to the temple court-yard and I shot a fire bolt into his chest, trying to disguise the way he had died. Lucifer left. I left. Raphael left. Waiting until the body would be discovered."

Michael's face was twisted with dread.

"I became fearful that we would all be exposed when you asked Mili Morningstar to investigate Gabriel's homicide. In a panic, I thought that maybe I could throw her off by condemning Lucifer. I knew that he would never tell and my case would be thrown out since the gun and all the other evidence was missing. But then Agatha Christie found out about where Mili Morningstar's Derringers were at and took it from there."

Michael looked at Agatha and then at Mili.

"I apologize for my shameful part in this whole affair, ladies. And I congratulate you on work well done. A brilliant partnership whose results stand for themselves." Michael paused, and then added a codicil. "Not that I will ever be a fan."

"I repent of the evil I have done," he continued. "I hurt you, and I hurt Raphael and Lucifer. I slaughtered the great and good Archangel Gabriel. I lied to you all. I tried to create a diversion by creating a stir over the deaths of three of my subordinates instead of declaring their deeds unworthy of any angel. I am sorry for all of these actions."

Michael looked Jehovah in the eye while he finished his confession. Then he fell to his knees with his head bowed. Lucifer and Raphael walked up next to him and went to their knees as well.

"We are all repentant," Raphael spoke. "But we are not seeking mercy. We accept responsibility for what we have done and are willing to submit to the justice you decide we deserve. We were created to serve you and we have failed. All we can say is that there is no excuse for our misdeeds."

Jehovah looked at the three Archangels, then addressed everyone in the room.

"You three Archangels stand condemned by the truth uncovered by Mili Morningstar, nee Wickett, Mardie Wickett, and Agatha Christie. I commend them for their work and thank them for a job that is now completed. It has once and for all time been revealed how and why Heaven lost Archangel Gabriel."

Mili felt herself begin to tremble. For all of Jehovah's aloofness, she could suddenly feel the overwhelming power he wielded. With the flick of his wrist, he could destroy Lucifer, and she would be left to mourn his loss for all eternity. She felt Mardie's arm around her waist. Agatha reached out and held her hand. Tears began to run down Mili's face.

"Hear my sentence," God declared. "Michael, you are relieved of your assignment. Raphael, you need some backbone. You will perform his duties. Michael will take your responsibility and we'll see if solitary time settles a heart that has grown entirely too violent.

"Lucifer, I am establishing a provisional period wherein you will assume Gabriel's assignment. You will receive a temporary restoration to the position and title of Archangel, representing me throughout the cosmos. You have successfully managed the damned. Let's see how you manage the living. For now, you will administer my righteous benevolence on Earth, in Heaven, and in Hell."

Jehovah smiled, clearly pleased with himself.

"Now if y'all don't mind, I'd like you to leave. I've missed two of my favorite television shows and that's enough for one day."

Goddamn, Mardie thought. Jehovah owns a curling iron, but not a DVR. Pathetic.

CHAPTER NINETEEN

After the audience with Jehovah, Raphael led everyone out of the temple and into the courtyard. Suddenly there was whooping and shouting and everyone was hugging and laughing. Lucifer hugged and kissed Mili over and over. Mardie deliberately positioned herself next to Charlton Heston and there was a lot of smooching and squeezing happening in their zone as well. Raphael and Michael shook hands, and both of them walked over to Agatha. Moments later Lucifer, holding Mili's hand, walked over and joined them.

"What is there to say?" Michael spoke first. "Mrs. Christie, you are unbelievable."

"I always felt that way about Archangels and God," she joked.

Raphael continued.

"We did such a tragic thing, killing our friend. Yet we were stuck as to how to deal with the tragedy. So, of course, we made everything worse."

Lucifer bowed his head respectfully.

"You saved us from ourselves," he said quietly. "Thank you."

Agatha smiled modestly.

"I only did the summing up, dear boy." She pointed her hand at Mili standing next to him. "You did the real work, Milicent." She looked over at Mardie who had her arm through Charlton's, locking him in place as it were. "You too, Mardell. Your love and support enabled Mili to see this investigation through."

She looked at the three Archangels.

"You lads must have very special places in God's heart. Instead of punishing you, he arranged for each of you to perform rehabilitating functions. I have never seen or heard of Jehovah doing such a thing before. How beautiful! It is exactly the kind of thing we have always expected of God. Love. Forgiveness. Renewal. How smashing that it happened here today."

Agatha shook her head in amazement.

"I never would have imagined what he had in store for *you,* Lucifer Morningstar. You have been given Gabriel's role, the Archangel spreading good tidings and blessings. While both Michael and Raphael will have to settle into their duties, you Lucifer, will instantly have the opportunity to do good a billion times a day throughout God's endless realm. May you be worthy of his trust."

Lucifer could not speak. Agatha knew in her heart exactly why he was terrified of the new role he had received. He was a fraud, a liar, and a greedy capitalist running the universe's greatest commercial empire using Hell's demons. He was impatient, violent, and unforgiving. Why had Jehovah laid this responsibility dispensing universal blessings on him?

Mili sensed her husband's unease and squeezed his hand. He looked at her. She mouthed I love you. How grateful that made him feel. She and their children had given him love and admiration. They had brought out whatever good qualities he had hidden deep in his heart for millennia. His wife and kids would see him through this, the greatest challenge he had ever faced.

Mili would love him. Little Mardie would give him grandkids. Sriracha would make him laugh. And cough. And he could train his son Jesus to be his replacement. There were only so many years he would be willing to do this new job and it would be good to hand it off to the single most righteous person he had ever met.

With hugs and promises to meet again, everyone went their own separate ways. For the time being. There was one future event that was destined to bind them and bring them all back together again. The first play scheduled for the premiere reenactment season in Heaven, *The Wickett Sisters in Hell*. Everyone swore on Jehovah's name that they would be there on opening night. Even God told Agatha that he would be attending and asked if she would sit by him. She was honored and was already calculating how to get a lock of his hair for Mili.

✳ ✳ ✳

It was a joyous night in Lucifer and Mili Morningstar's townhome. The Devil recounted a blow-by-blow account of the historic meeting with Jehovah. He gave credit to Mili for the hard work of chasing the clues to find Archangel Gabriel's killer. He mentioned Mardie's sturdy and abiding loyalty in helping see Mili through the brutal case. And he acknowledged Agatha's crowning contribution in summing up the evidence and pointing the accusing finger at all three Archangels.

Little Mardie seemed particularly affected by Gabriel's ignominious death. Sad and embarrassing. And so unnecessary. Yet she was wonderfully glad that her father had not personally held the gun or pulled the trigger. Sriracha tried to imagine what it had been like for the four most powerful angels in Creation to be sitting around playing poker. Who won? And who lost? Besides Gabriel?

Jesus was pleased that his father had been forgiven and promoted. Good out of evil. Love out of tragedy. A bright future born from a dark deed. He didn't care what anybody thought about Jehovah. God was his hero. The king of the universe moved in mysterious ways, his wonders to perform. Why he himself possessed an innate love and appreciation for all things divine, Jesus did not know. But he would not change for the world. Or for Hell. Maybe for Heaven.

Mili grilled ribeye steaks, made Caesar salad, and served fresh-baked rolls from the local Hells Bells. The store had even begun to stock a wide variety of pipe tobaccos in honor of its famous customer, Albert Einstein. Mili had run into the professor when she had shopped today. He was opening various packages of tobacco and smoking a bit of each.

They chatted happily while Dr. Einstein puffed his way through Jester, Dunhill, and Warhorse tobaccos. All was well with Hugh Everett III, he told Mili. The great quantum physicist was living an alternate life of great happiness with his wife, son, and daughter. And not just in his parallel world, Einstein added, but in multiple worlds all over the galaxies as well. Many happy returns to all of hims, Mili said. Albert didn't get it.

At dinner she served Lucifer a great big steak. Sriracha got an out-sized one as well. Little Mardie took only a sliver of steak and focused on an entrée-size Caesar salad. Jesus asked for a vegetarian steak. Mili served him a nice juicy ribeye thinking that was exactly what he was asking for. It was.

There was a lot of laughing and talking all through the meal. And why not? Lucifer had been judged for dead. And yet he was alive. He had been lost. But now he was found. Prodigal Archangel, indeed. Late that night together in bed, Mili shared a few words that she'd saved up to say to her husband.

"Don't ever do that to me again, Lucifer Morningstar," she said accusingly.

"What, love?" her husband asked, instantly worried.

"Don't ever *lie* to me again. Not ever."

"I apologize. I truly do. I only did it to save the Archangels from God's wrath."

"And to save your own ass from God's boot," Mili responded.

"That, too. I admit it. Never again though. I promise."

"All right," Mili told him. "Now that that's out of the way, I must tell you that your return to the ranks of the Archangels is stupendous!"

"I hope so," Lucifer answered. "Yet I always thought I was serving God down here."

"Oh!" Mili groaned. "Such bullshit. You've spent thousands of years building the greatest moneymaking business the universe has ever seen. You probably own every major shipping company in the universe and have exclusive use of every trading route that traverses Hell, Earth, and Heaven. I would guess that millions upon millions of demons work every day across all twenty billion galaxies to make you even richer." Mili looked the Devil right in the eye. "I found out lots of things about you up in Heaven."

"Well," Satan responded, "if it is any comfort to you, in taking on Gabriel's duties my ownership in various import/export businesses—whatever they may be—will be held in blind trusts, and their day-to-day operations will be handled by my senior managers. I will not be involved at all. *My* attention will turn to serving goodness throughout Creation. That will be my fulltime job."

"With time scheduled for your family," Mili added. "Plus buying Pfot a new car to drive us around, *and* building a new house for me and the children."

"Ha!" Lucifer laughed. "Good one!"

"I'm serious! You're going to do all of those things. Right away."

Satan was silent for a moment.

"That new house, by the way," Mili continued, "will be flanked by guest houses for Mardie, Agatha, and if he likes, Charlton Heston."

"Done," Lucifer declared firmly, and placed his hand over his heart.

Mili hugged her husband and gave him a long kiss. She'd said all that she had intended to say. That didn't mean she was ready to go to sleep, however.

✳ ✳ ✳

169

It was opening night at the Wickett Sisters Reenactment Club in Heaven. The audience was seated, drinks had been served, and the lights were dimmed. Two large square tables had been pulled together in front for Mili and Mardie, honored as special guests, with seats for Charlton Heston, Agatha Christie, the Archangels Michael, Raphael, and Lucifer, and Jehovah himself.

The ladies were wearing black evening gowns, dress jewelry, and high heels. The Archangels were wearing metallic-silver robes with gold wire trim at the neck, sleeves, and bottom hem. Jehovah had on a new black tuxedo, a fancy white dress shirt, and a black bow tie. His long black hair had been pulled into a thick, wavy ponytail. His appearance made it obvious that he'd been watching some old movies on TV. His face looked the same as Charlton Heston seated just down from him.

It has been several weeks since God had decreed the changes in Heaven's hierarchy. Michael had become noticeably more relaxed and spent his leisure time getting manicures and enjoying avant-garde graphic novels from Drawn and Quarterly Press in Montreal. He was into one right now by Chester Brown, *Mary Wept Over the Feet of Jesus*. He was reading and realizing for the first time in his long life that truth came in endless shades of gray. It was causing him to change his views on everything.

Taking on Michael's old responsibilities, Raphael had reduced the number of divine punishments by more than ninety-nine percent. Executions had been eliminated completely and replaced by Raphael appearing in heavenly glory—fiery sword and all—exhorting evil-doers in their dreams. He chastised them and warned of terrible consequences if they did not repent of the evil tempting them. Sort of scared straight for those who were just a step away from murder, kidnapping, and rape.

It worked, largely because people tended to take their nightmares seriously. Granted, this was not exactly what God had had in mind when he had assigned Michael's duties to Raphael. But who could argue with the results? A lot less people were going to Hell for sure.

Lucifer spent a lot of time traveling through the cosmos. While he had never been deeply into the affairs of all the various worlds, he had certainly known where and how to make money on each of them. His duties now required being aware of the needs of God's children and coming to their aid. He listened to prayers and he answered them for the countless folk who had their faith in God's goodness. Jehovah was pleased. Best therapy by far for the Archangel who had tried to drive him from his throne. Though he *still* wouldn't spend time alone with Lucifer anywhere.

Charlton Heston and Mardie had become a couple. After years of dating Bowles—the handsome bartender at the reenactment club in Hell—Mardie had moved on. Charlton was intelligent, kind, and knew how to put on a mean BBQ. Maybe it was just love in first bloom, but both of them were enormously happy, whether reading Mardie's poetry, or practicing with guns at the SHOOT! firing range.

Agatha Christie had become friends with God. He admired her mind and had begun reading her mysteries. He quite enjoyed discussing them with her, and proudly told how early into each book he guessed the ending. Except for her most famous mystery of all, *Then There Were None*. He admitted that she had stumped him. He congratulated her—albeit a bit stiffly—and asked her why she wasn't writing mysteries up in Heaven. I've turned to playwriting, she told him, then grinned. Who do you think is doing the adaptations of the Wickett sisters' adventures?

Mili and Lucifer were adjusting to his new role and frequent travel. Things in Hell were running well enough that he could direct his attention elsewhere. He was actually surprised how nice things had become and how smoothly things were going in the underworld, especially compared to the chaos everywhere else. Much of the credit went to David Ben-Gurion and Moshe Dayan at the Ben-Yehuda Kibbutz. Maybe in the future he would turn Hell into a democracy and encourage them to run for office. Prime Minister Ben-Gurion? It had a nice ring to it.

Pfotenhauer was driving Mili and the children around in a new Tesla Model S coupe. Lucifer refused to ride in it, preferring his new Prius and his Harley-Davidson motorcycle. Was he being petulant? Mili decided not to care. She had gotten her new automobile. And her new house.

She had asked for and gotten an exact copy of Zane Gray's rambling Pueblo-style summer mansion built on Santa Catalina Island, twenty-three miles off the Pacific coast from Los Angeles. She loved Zane Gray's fishing books (and hated his western novels) and made a visit with Little Mardie to see his own gorgeous house set on a hill overlooking Catalina's Bay of the Seven Moons.

In another life she would have liked to have been Zane's secretary sailing the seas on his one-hundred-and-ninety-foot three-masted schooner, *The Fisherman*. But now she settled on having him over to the house down here in Hell for whiskey and talk, which consisted largely of his reminisces about fishing. And books. And women. He was still a bit fresh considering he'd dropped dead of heart failure at the age of sixty-seven. Just worn out. Not *entirely* worn out he told her, winking.

The lights went dark in the theater, then back up. The play's first scene was beginning with Mardie (Bette Davis, old and gorgeous) going to the hospital down in Hell to meet Mili (Joan Crawford, old and scary). An off-stage narrator spoke of the twin sisters' long estrangement, and the reason for the unlikely reunion of Mardie in Hell and Mili from Heaven; Satan asked them to solve Hell's first murder.

Mardie walked into Mili's hospital room on stage as the real Mardie and Mili looked at each other across the table at the club. How naïve they had been. How angry with each other they had felt. How lucky they were to have been given another chance. They smiled at each other. Then they leaned back in their chairs and watched the show.

Epilogue

Not long after the reenactment evening, Mili received a small package from Agatha Christie couriered down from Heaven. Inside was a small, zipped, clear plastic baggie with a locket of black hair. There was no note or explanation. There didn't need to be.

The End

Acknowledgements

I would like to thank my wonderful friends and faithful readers!

Sabrina Ambrose

Margie Cleland

Peter R. Haggard

Bobette Jones

Trace Jones

Per Kvalheim

Dr. Vladimir Khapchik

Rose Myers

Sheridan Oakes

Lorraine M. Petrakis

Lloyd Russell

Nicholas Saman

Elizabeth Wagner

Linda White